UNCONVENTIONAL LOVE

COLLECTION #29

MEYARI MCFARLAND

CONTENTS

Special Offer	v
Other Books by Meyari McFarland:	vii
Author's Note: The Girl of Silver Clouds	1
Housewarming	2
Labor Day	10
Halloween	17
Thanksgiving	25
Christmas	32
Author's Note: The Absence of Wrath	40
The Absence of Wrath	41
Author's Note: Dandelion Intrigues	52
Dandelion Intrigues	53
Author's Note: Pink Trucks and Bow Ties	62
Pink Trucks and Bow Ties	63
Author's Note: Theorem of Bright Half-Light	82
Theorem of Bright Half-Light	83
Author's Note: The Billionaire's Kidnapped Beauty	94
1. Pike's Place Market	95
2. Room Service	103
Other Books by Meyari McFarland:	113
Afterword	115
Author Bio	116

SPECIAL OFFER

The rainbow has infinite shades, just as this collection covers the spectrum of fictional possibilities.

From contemporary romances like *The Shores of Twilight Bay* to dark fantasy like *A Lone Red Tree* and out to SF futures in *Child of Spring*, *Iridescent* covers the gamut of time, space and genre.

Meyari McFarland shows her mastery in this first omnibus collection of her short fiction. Twenty-five amazing stories, all with queer characters going on adventures, solving mysteries, and falling in love are here in the first Rainbow Collection.

And now you can get this massive collection of short queer fiction, all of it with the happy endings you love, *for free!*

Sign up here for your free copy of Iridescent now!

OTHER BOOKS BY MEYARI MCFARLAND:

Day Hunt on the Final Oblivion
Day of Joy
Immortal Sky

A New Path
Following the Trail
Crafting Home
Finding a Way
Go Between
Like Arrows of Fate

Out of Disaster

The Shores of Twilight Bay

Coming Together
Following the Beacon
The Solace of Her Clan

You can find these and many other books at www.MDR-Publishing.com. We are a small independent publisher focusing on LGBT content. Please sign up for our mailing list to get regular updates on the latest preorders and new releases and a free ebook!

Copyright ©2024 by Mary Raichle

Print ISBN: 978-1-64309-123-5

Cover image

© Mo_Ali on DepositPhoto ID# 310719988

All rights reserved. No part of this publication may be reproduced or transmitted in any form or by any means, electronic or mechanical, including photocopy, recording or any information storage and retrieval system, without permission in writing from the publisher.

Requests for permission to make copies of any part of the work should be emailed to publisher@mdr-publishing.com.

This book is also available in TPB format from all major retailers.

❀ Created with Vellum

This collection is dedicated to my parents, the first love I saw and still one of the best romances I've ever known.

AUTHOR'S NOTE: THE GIRL OF SILVER CLOUDS

A collection focused on unconventional romances had to start with this story. Normally I would have put it last as the anchor for the collection but not this time. For this collection, it has to start with Caron going through the seasons as she finds herself and forges a love with the last person anyone would have expected, including her.

Neurodivergence and queer relationships mix with trauma and growing up to create a story that perfectly fit this theme. Enjoy!

HOUSEWARMING

Caron bit her lip as her roommate Refilwe paused on the sidewalk leading up to Tiyamike's house. Music boomed even though the windows and door were closed. Seriously, it was like being outside of a bar though it was three in the afternoon instead of eleven at night. Just with less smoke, thank goodness.

It was a nice house in a nice neighborhood, a nice white picket fence surrounding a nicely trimmed lawn and nice shrubs that were trimmed and cute and everything that fit into the neighborhood. Until you noticed that the neighboring houses had their curtains firmly drawn. Almost aggressively drawn. Caron saw the curtains on the house to the right twitch.

A very white woman glared at her.

Oh great. The cops were definitely going to get called. Soon. They needed to turn that music down, pronto. Not that Tiyamike would care. Her dad was a cop and he'd already said, apparently, that he'd make sure they didn't get any trouble. Nice for Tiyamike, not so good for Caron who he barely knew.

"Man, this is great," Refilwe exclaimed. She bounced on her toes, giggling like a pre-teen. "It's such a cute little house!"

So strange to see a big black body builder giggling like that but it was Refilwe. She'd never cared what anyone thought about her. Being so big gave her that advantage, mostly. Wouldn't matter if a cop car drove by but maybe they could run for the front door? Tiyamike might be able to call her father, get the cops to back off before someone got shot.

"We really shouldn't be here," Caron said, stomach in knots. "Come on, we should go home, Refilwe. It's not a good idea."

"Oh nonsense," Refilwe said. She tugged Caron towards the front steps, all three of them. Caron wasn't used to so few stairs, so unlike the row houses she'd grown up with. "I know you're anxious about it but you know everyone."

"Not the neighbors," Caron hissed as she twisted her wrist to get free. Unsuccessfully. "They're going to call the cops. This isn't the sort of neighborhood where we can be safe, Refilwe. You know it's not."

Refilwe sighed and tugged hard, pulling Caron right up next to her side. Her arm was a beefy iron bar around Caron's shoulders as she pointed to the house on the right where Caron had seen the white woman.

"Sweetie, that gal's disabled," Refilwe said. "Tiyamike brings her food at least every other day. She's got massive anxiety and can't talk to people without panic attacks. Nice lady apparently, just seriously unable to go out between the need for a walker and her agoraphobia. Doesn't help that her idiot son won't put in a ramp for her. Tiyamike and Duri had to carry her out of the house the last time she had a doctor's appointment."

Caron stared at the determinedly curtain-covered window, then at Refilwe. "Oh."

"Now," Refilwe said, pointing at the house on the left,

"they're apparently this super-cool old Asian couple who travel all over the world. They're not even home right now. They're off in Peru seeing Manchu Picchu, hiking up by food the way the Peruvians used to. Won't be back for a month. Tiyamike is watering their plants. Across the street is three houses with young families, none of whom are home at this time of day. We're fine."

"Oh."

It wasn't... This wasn't a dangerous neighborhood. As respectable as the houses looked, this wasn't someplace that would get her killed just for walking around. Normal people, nice people, instead of rich old white men and women who would look down on her just for her dark skin, her thousands of freckles all across her body, her mop of curly hair that would never, ever behave.

Tiyamike's neighborhood was safe.

Her legs shook with the release of the nervous energy. That stubborn part of her mind that always took the worst-case scenario stubbornly insisted that Refilwe couldn't possibly be right about it. But she didn't lie about things like that. Especially when Caron was on the verge of panic attacks.

Refilwe had been her touchstone of reality every since they met. She'd never betrayed Caron yet. Thank goodness. Caron wasn't sure she'd still be alive if she didn't have someone to help her navigate the paranoia and anxiety.

"Okay," Caron mumbled. "Sorry."

"Eh, it's okay, sweetie." Refilwe grinned. "Let's get in there and party!"

She all but picked Caron up as she hurried up the stairs and pounded on the door. Caron opened her mouth to protest but the door flew open and there was Tiyamike, her hair flying in the longest afro possible, dress as bright as a rainbow. With all the colors of a rainbow, for that matter.

It was short and tight, showing off all of Tiyamike's ample curves. Sleeveless too, which would have kept Caron in the bathroom because god, she wouldn't have been able to let anyone see her upper arms. Tiyamike didn't seem to notice that her saggy triceps were right there for everyone to see as she grinned at the two of them.

"You made it!" Tiyamike exclaimed. "Come on in, you two. Everyone else is here. Duri's making burgers out back. Jun and Nkruma are upstairs doing something. I'm not asking what and I recommend you don't either. Azar's the one in charge of the music, Caron, so if it's too much, you just say so. Azar will turn it down. Oh, and I've got a friend from home visiting, Sabah Gensch. She's... Huh. Probably hiding somewhere. She gets nervous meeting new people."

Caron nodded, trying to find words to say thank you and sorry and oh god, not a new person to meet. All that came out was a garbled little sound, not that it seemed to bother Tiyamike. She just hugged Caron and then laughed as Refilwe lifted her right off her feet when they hugged.

It was a cute house, loud music notwithstanding. Azar nodded to Caron as she turned the music down, shifting from a pounding rock beat to a quieter instrumental with soothing flutes and violins. Caron's shoulders relaxed immediately. Of course, Azar didn't say anything. She never did, preferring to sit with the music instead of interacting with the people directly. Her hoodie, black as always, was pulled up over her head so it was a bad day for her, too, where interaction would overload her.

Caron slipped away from Tiyamike and Refilwe's enthusiastic discussion of which dips were best with corn chips versus potato chips, dodging into the kitchen where Duri stood with a tray of cooked hamburger patties while Kaede, tall and thin and constantly moving to the beat of Azar's music, put together what looked like a hundred sliders.

"Pickle chips, yes or no?" Kaede asked. She glanced towards Caron.

"Um, I prefer them but maybe some without?" Caron suggested. "There's someone new?"

"Sabah," Duri said, nodding towards the back yard. "She's outside. Too many new people. You going to go stare or hide with her?"

"I'd hide upstairs but Tiyamike said that might not be a good idea."

Both Kaede and Duri rolled their eyes, synchronized even, so no, not a good idea. Caron took two sliders, a bottle of water and then cautiously slipped outside. She didn't seen anyone immediately but that didn't say anything.

Tiyamike and Duri didn't believe in perfectly manicured yards. They had complained about it a million times before they bought this house. So Caron wasn't surprised that the back yard had bushes in huge pots, several big old trees that shaded the whole thing and a lovely little picnic area complete with a table near the door. And a grill, standing open and quietly ticking in the afternoon sunshine.

She looked around again and then shivered as she sat at the table with her sliders. Well, whoever Sabah was, apparently she was even worse at new people than Caron was. Caron couldn't see her anywhere.

Eating helped. A lot. It generally did. There was something hugely grounding about the taste and texture of food. Cleansing about the water rinsing her teeth clean. Caron sighed once she was done.

She should go back inside.

Everyone else was inside. Doing their own things. Which meant that Caron was permitted, no, required, to do what made her feel most comfortable. Tiyamike's Golden Rule: Everyone has a comfort zone and they were all required to seek it when they were uncomfortable around her.

Going back inside wasn't good. Maybe she could sit next to Azar but with Azar overloaded, no, that wouldn't work. Hiding upstairs wouldn't work, either, not with Jun and Nkruma being obnoxious lovers again. So yard it was.

Caron drummed her fingers against the table. Stopped. Spread her hands flat on it. Stopped that too because pressing so hard hurt her wrist. Stood. Sat. Stood again. Her legs shook so hard that she had to sit down again.

"Nervous?"

The voice came from behind the nearest huge potted bush, a big lilac planted in a brilliantly teal pot that came up to Caron's chin.

"Oh, please don't hide," Caron begged. "I get paranoid about people spying on me."

Her whole body was shaking now, damn it. Stupid paranoia. Stupid anxiety attacks. Her heart pounded so hard that the world swam and wobbled around her. Everything out here could hide a threat. Lots of threats. Cops and men and judgmental neighbors and...

No. No. It wasn't that bad. Refilwe had told her. She'd promised. It was Tiyamike's home. It wasn't dangerous here. It was safe. It was.

Caron found herself with her knees pressed against her chest, breath coming in pants, and realized as she moved and stretched aching arms, trembling legs, that it'd been several minutes.

There was a young woman, about Caron's age, sitting on the other side of the picnic table from her. She was cute. Pretty, really. Instead of Caron's horribly spotty skin, Sabah had rich brown skin the color of late, late sunset, red and brown with hints of gold across her cheekbones, nose and lips. Her hair was lovely, too, long and sleek, as straight as a ruler, pure black.

Her shirt was the color of clouds after a rain when the

sky was going back to bright blue, silver-white, soft and billowing around her body. She looked like a tree with a silver cloud wrapped around it.

"Sorry," Caron whispered.

"It's okay," Sabah said in a strangely flat voice. Her hands were tucked into her lap, out of sight, but the set of her shoulders and the tightness of her upper arms made Caron think she was nervous, too. "I had a panic attack earlier, too. That's why I'm out here."

Caron smiled, more than a little bitterly. "Tiyamike likes gathering up the wounded ones."

Sabah nodded back. "She always has. I think she enjoys protecting people. Are the sliders good?"

That wasn't what Caron had expected to be said next. Most people asked why. Why are you so anxious? Why are you so afraid? You're so young. You have so much to look forward to. Smile! Just buck up, smile more, eat more yoghurt, do Yoga, you'll feel so much better.

Stupid.

Malfunctioning brains didn't need yoga.

"Um, yeah?" Caron said. "I don't... necessarily taste them. It's the texture that helps for me. But the pickles tasted good. Nice and crispy. Sweet."

"Flaky biscuit buns or doughy buns?" Sabah asked, once again surprising Caron by not asking all the normal stupid questions about how you could eat but not taste things.

"Er. Flaky? I think they're actually biscuits."

Sabah nodded. She frowned towards the door, breathing so slowly and deliberately that Caron realized that she was working herself up to going inside for some for herself. Well, that Caron could help with. Not much else but that she could do.

"Um, do you want company?" Caron asked. She blushed as Sabah stared at her. "Normally I spend time with Azar.

She's non-verbal, communicates in music and texting. It's. Well. Easier. But she's got her hood up so she's overloaded. And my roommate Refilwe and Tiyamike are doing their talking about all the things as fast and as loud as they can thing. That's stressful. Duri and Kaede are probably going around to make sure everyone eats. Duri cooks when she's stressed. And when she's happy. Kaede mothers everyone."

"And the other two are upstairs," Sabah said, still with a very calm, very flat tone.

Such an odd inflection to use, especially with panic attacks. Perhaps she was autistic? Or partially deaf? Not that it mattered. Given that she was Tiyamike's friend, Sabah was likely as different as the rest of them, just in her own way.

"Yes."

"Please," Sabah said, no intonation at all but her eyes looked like it was a desperate plea.

Caron tried a smile. It felt shaky but the fear in Sabah's eyes eased so it must be good enough. She nodded, one hand pressed hard against the picnic table. Her legs didn't want to support her.

"All right," Caron said. "Forgive me if I'm a bit slow."

Sabah's lips twitched into a smile for a second before going back to normal. "Forgiven."

They made their way back inside together, Sabah carrying Caron's plate and water bottle.

LABOR DAY

"This is going to be amazing," Refilwe said as she carefully lifted the cupcakes out of the back seat.

Laughter rang out from the back yards across the street. Small children's laughter. Grown up laugher. Lots of laughter. Caron bit her lip and did her best not to scan the street for pedophiles. There were no pedophiles in the neighborhood. No one was going to come and hurt the kids.

Just like no, cops weren't going to come and attack them for parking in front of Tiyamike and Duri's house. It wasn't going to happen. No matter how much her paranoia whispered at her that yes, it definitely was.

Refilwe's voice was muffled by the huge box of cupcakes she was carrying. Caron still wasn't sure how she'd managed to get four dozen cupcakes into one box, all without using those plastic carrying boxes they had at the grocery store. But she had.

Caron had the potato salad and a huge bottle of lemonade for the party. Tiyamike and Duri had declared last week that any Labor Day celebrations had to be held at their house this year.

Most of the time, in the past anyway, they'd gone to a public park and risked sensory overload (Azar), inappropriate kissing (Jun and Nkruma could never resist making people stare), panic attacks (Caron, still, despite her new meds), and ants.

At least at Tiyamike's they didn't have to worry about the ants. That would be a very nice improvement over the last few years. Caron was honestly looking forward to having potato salad and sandwiches without ants crawling all over them. The door opened before Caron even climbed the three steps up to Tiyamike's porch. She blinked because it was Sabah who held the door open for them.

"I thought you went back to Missoula," Caron said to Sabah.

"I did," Sabah agreed in her monotone voice. "To pack. I have a job here now."

"Oh, nice!" Refilwe said, peering out from behind her box of cupcakes. "You get two cupcakes then. Or you know, as many as you want. I brought lots. Thanks for holding the door, Sabah."

She breezed right past both of them, calling out hello's to everyone else. The music hadn't started so obviously Azar wasn't there yet. Caron found herself blushing as Sabah stared at her so fixedly that it made her heart beat faster. Hard to tell if it was fear or embarrassment that made her quiver this way. But there was nothing to fear.

Sabah had never, in the entire month or so that Caron had known her, touched her without permission. Explicit, verbal permission each time. There was no threat there. None at all. So it must be embarrassment and maybe something like attraction because really, Sabah was quite pretty despite her very flat affect.

She had silver earrings shaped like clouds today. Her shirt was blue and green, a Seahawks shirt. It hung loose enough around her body that Caron couldn't see curves. Which was fine. Sabah had to be comfortable in it.

Though it would be nice if she'd stop staring quite so hard.

"You should come in," Sabah said.

"Yes, I know, sorry," Caron said, blushing even harder. She bobbed her head and edged past Sabah and then huffed at herself. "Sorry. I just. Damn it."

"You're allowed to touch people," Sabah said with just a hint of emotion in her voice.

Caron stared at her, the still warm air outside billowing in because she was standing right in the middle of the doorway. She moved inside. Sabah closed the door, still watching Caron just a hair too closely for her nerves.

"I was just reminding myself of that," Caron admitted. "Sorry. I um. I get very. Nervous. About touching. And everything else. When I'm startled."

"I do that too," Sabah said, nodding calmly. "Jun and Nkruma are in the back yard making a bonfire. A small one. Azar said that she'd be late in her text. Kaede is... making something very complicated in the kitchen."

Caron blinked and then grinned. She could hear Tiyamike and Refilwe talking fast and furious about frosting, baking and flavors in the hallway. Probably to Duri who loved cupcakes with an unholy passion but wouldn't make them for herself.

"Thank you," Caron said. "It helps to know where everyone is and how they're feeling."

"I appreciated it when you did it for me," Sabah said. She held her hands out for the potato salad so Caron passed it over. "Tell me if something else will help."

Caron stared at her, just as hard as Sabah stared at her. After a minute or so Sabah's cheeks went faintly pink. Huh. Maybe she wasn't interpreting that stare the right way. She'd thought that perhaps Sabah's emotions were as flat as her voice but it didn't seem that way. Not as Sabah shifted her feet and blushed.

"What does it mean when you stare at me?" Caron asked, leaning against the wall right next to the front door.

"That... I think you're beautiful?" Sabah said and there was a distinct question in her tone this time. Not a loud question but still a question.

"Why did I ask?" Caron asked. "Or you're not sure if I'm beautiful?"

"Oh, no, you're definitely beautiful," Sabah said as if the was the most self-evident thing anyone had ever said throughout all time and space. "I didn't know why you asked."

Caron sighed and gestured for Sabah to come with her. They dropped off the potato salad and lemonade. She made appropriately impressed noises as Kaede explained her very complicated dinner that involved stuffing wrapped with pounded flat pork chops wrapped in prosciutto cooked with some sort of complicated crust that was gluten and nut free out of respect for Azar's digestive issues. And then she slipped away to go upstairs with Sabah on her heels.

The upstairs had two rooms. A bedroom with a beautiful king bed that Tiyamike and Duri shared. And a lovely little office / sitting room with a comfy love seat and a big lounge chair that Caron immediately claimed. Sabah sat on the love seat, her feet tucked under her and a pillow hugged to her chest.

"I ask about stuff like that because I don't... see the same world as everyone else," Caron explained. Or didn't quite explain from the puzzled look in Sabah's eyes. "I have anxiety, clinical, so I see problems where there really aren't problems. Lots of them. And they're always bigger than they actually are. And then I have paranoia, medicated of course, so I tend to take every little look and gesture as a threat. Refilwe. Um. She's my touch stone. She tells me what she sees whenever I ask so that I can know that I'm either seeing things accurately or blowing them out of proportion."

"That's nice," Sabah said. She blinked rapidly several times before leaning back into the love seat. "I stare because I think you're beautiful and way out of my league. And because I don't actually enjoy sex. So staring is all that I'd want."

"Really?" Caron asked, surprised that someone would admit it so openly. "Tiyamike gave me a huge lecture on sex and gender and orientation shortly after I met her. But I wasn't. Well. I thought she was diagnosing me with things instead of just giving me information."

Sabah's lips quirked in a microsecond smile again. "She does that to everyone."

Caron nodded. She'd learned that since but at the time it had been terrifying and so very strange. Now, it was a kindness. The more time she spent around Tiyamike and her friends, the easier it was to identify her own emotions underneath her anxiety and paranoia.

"I never have had anyone just tell me outright that they were interested in me before," Caron observed. She smiled and sighed, tucking her knees to her chest. "They just get angry when I don't realize that they've been flirting all along. Normally I see it as a threat."

"Not a threat," Sabah instantly said. She blinked once, slowly. "Are you interested in me?"

Caron's cheeks went hot. Very hot. "Um, yeah. You're lovely. Stunning really. And um. Just saying things outright? That's very helpful for me to cope."

"I wish the whole world would just say things openly," Sabah said with a little huff of air that might be a sigh. If it was stronger. Louder.

It would be nice. Caron smiled as she tried to imagine

dating Sabah. Hard to picture because she knew so little about Sabah. Nothing about why she talked that way, why she was prone to panic attacks. What her job was or where she was living. Her favorite food and color and childhood pets.

She wanted to know, though. Caron had relaxed faster around Sabah than she had with anyone else in the world so far. Even Refilwe had had to work very hard indeed to get Caron to calm down and listen. Still did, honestly.

"Talk to me?" Caron asked. Sabah's stare went shocked. "Tell me about yourself a little, please? I um. Want to know you better. And spend more time with you. You're calming. Soothing. I mean, you don't have to if you don't want to but I'd like…"

"To date?" Sabah asked, her shoulders relaxing as she played with the pillow on her lap, fluffing it and smoothing the wrinkles perfectly flat.

"Yes," Caron said. She wrinkled her nose and smiled, nervous and hopeful all at once. "If you want. Sex gives me panic attacks. There was. Stuff. When I was younger. So there's no problem with your asexuality. I just. You're pretty. And you're forthright. And you like me, too. So. Um. Do you want to date me?"

"I do," Sabah said with the firmest infection that Caron had heard from her yet. "What do you want to know?"

Everything seemed like far too much so Caron shrugged. "Um. Tell me about your childhood pets? If you had any, of course."

Sabah's eyes sparkled with laughter. Joy maybe. The corners of her eyes wrinkled as her lips twitched upwards at the corners. Most of her expression really was in her eyes. How interesting. They were lovely eyes, too, grey as a storm cloud. Caron settled in on the lounge chair and listened as Sabah started talking about her childhood dog, Moby Dog.

It felt like a start though Caron wasn't sure what it would end up being. At least the office room was quiet and calm. She could hear the others talking downstairs so she felt. Huh. Safe. Protected. Like home.

Sitting with Sabah, listening to her talk and to the others go about their business downstairs, felt like home. Caron smiled.

Yes. This would probably end badly but for now it was nice. Even if they only dated for a few days or weeks, Caron was glad she'd explained and then asked.

HALLOWEEN

*T*iyamike's porch was decorated with smiling jack-o-lanterns. Three of them. One was an actual pumpkin that had been carved. The other two were plastic lamps that shone light over the steps and sidewalk. Unlike her neighbors, Tiyamike had kept her decorations light-hearted, cheerful, non-scary in the extreme.

Ms. Anderson to the right had no decorations at all. Caron wasn't surprised by that. She didn't want guests or visitors so of course not. The Nguyens to the left had every decoration in the world. Their house looked like a truly haunted house even though last weekend it'd looked perfectly normal.

"It's not real," Sabah said, one hand gently touching Caron's elbow.

"I know," Caron said. "I don't understand why such nice people want to be so scary."

"Eh, they're playing at it one night of the year," Refilwe said as she locked her car up. "They can play with it and set it aside, go back to normal life after that."

It seemed unfair. None of them got to pretend that they

were normal. Why did other people get to pretend to be strange?

Caron took Sabah's hand, let her lead Caron up into Tiyamike's house past the big bowl of full size candy bars that Tiyamike and Duri would be passing out to trick or treaters. If they got any. So few kids went trick or treating door to door anymore. Everyone knew it wasn't as safe as going to the mall.

So maybe they'd be taking the candy bars home with them after Tiyamike's Halloween party. Which looked to be in full swing. Refilwe ran upstairs, leaving them behind. A moment or so later, Caron heard Refilwe start chattering to Kaede about her costume.

While the outside had some decorations, the inside had none. Caron appreciated that. Spiders and bats the size of her head in unexpected places scared her for days sometimes. She'd be very glad when Halloween was over and everything went back to normal.

Azar was at the stereo, tailoring the music to the people dancing in the living room. She'd dressed like Wednesday Adams, but with a hoody. The hood was done today so she was having a good day. That was nice. Jun and Nkruma were actually there, dancing together like it was a slow tune even though the beat was fairly fast.

Apparently the three of them had decided on an Adam's Family theme because Jun was dressed like Gomez, including a fake mustache, but with the jacket off and sleeves rolled up to the elbow. Nkruma was a very lovely Morticia, just with dark skin instead of pasty. It worked. Quite well. Better than Caron's half-hearted mermaid dress. At least Sabah looked good dressed as Black Widow. She had a perfect figure for Black Widow's catsuit. Though Sabah zipped the suit all the way up to her chin instead of showing off cleavage.

It looked better that way, more realistic.

June and Nkruma looked very happy. Jun had a new tattoo on her arm, a peony to go with the lily, rose, tulip and wisteria she'd already gotten. Soon she'd have a full sleeve tattoo. And Nkruma's grin as they danced was bright and happy. She'd taken off her dark glasses so that the ruin where her eyes used to be was visible.

No strangers here tonight then.

"I've never seen her eyes before," Sabah commented, quietly, to Caron.

"There was a car accident," Caron said, slowly pulling Sabah towards the kitchen where she could hear Duri and Tiyamike bickering about something. "She nearly died. Nkruma met Jun in physical therapy. She was there to help a friend of hers."

"That's nice," Sabah said.

The argument between Duri and Tiyamike was a little one. They were smiling as they tried to decide if the Jell-O mold of brains was ready to remove from it's mold. Caron relaxed a little seeing it. Good. It wasn't something that would tear Tiyamike and Duri apart.

"If it's firm to the touch it should be ready," Sabah said to Tiyamike and Duri.

"Hey, you made it," Tiyamike said with her biggest smile. "Yeah, it's close. But not quite. We're just worried about it freezing if we leave it in the freezer much longer."

"Fridge," Duri said, nodding welcome to both of them.

Tiyamike had a huge witch's hat on over one of her normal dresses. She'd put her afro into twists that came down to her waist, dark against the bright of her dress. Granted it was one with a black background for the bright geometric designs but it was still an every-day dress for her. Duri, on the other hand, had dressed just like Tiyamike. She had a bright tunic, floofy pants and she'd even wrapped her hair in a neon green and gold scarf so that she had a turban on her head. It made her head look twice the actual size.

"You look good," Caron said before she could overthink it.

Duri smiled so brightly that Caron immediately blushed and edged behind Sabah. Who let her. Thank goodness. Caron's heart beat faster as her paranoia shouted that Tiyamike was going to be mad at her for hitting on Duri.

"Thank you!" Duri said. "I wanted to wear the outfit Tiya's family gave me but most of the time I just don't have the occasion for it. This is what I'm planning on wearing to our wedding."

"Isn't it gorgeous?" Tiyamike said, bouncing on her toes and clapping her hands. "I'm so glad you guys like it. We had it made special just for Duri."

"It looks very good," Sabah said in her normal flat tone but with just a bit more emphasis that Caron was learning meant that she was trying her best to distract people from Caron's panic attack so it wouldn't get worse.

Which was so sweet that Caron gently wrapped her arms around Sabah's waist. She stayed there through Sabah's start of surprise, her slight stiffening and to that moment when Sabah relaxed back against her. Hugs had been right. Good. Caron was learning.

"You two look really good, too," Duri said with that approving mom look she got when one of them did something right. "I love your mermaid dress, Caron."

"It's nothing special," Caron said only to stop as Duri shook her head sternly and Sabah huffed.

"That's a compliment," Sabah said. "Your therapist said you have to say thank you and accept the compliment even if you don't think you deserve it."

"I like this therapist," Duri said, grinning at Caron as she whined and blushed. "Come on. I'm waiting for my thank you."

Caron huffed at them, hiding her face in Sabah's shoulder before working up the nerve to mumble 'thank you' against Sabah's shoulder.

"She said thank you," Sabah translated for Caron. Her hands rested over Caron's, warm and comforting even if Sabah couldn't really make her inflections work the way everyone else's did.

"Good enough for me," Duri said much to Caron's relief. "You two willing to help us get things set up for the buffet table? Other than the brains, everything is pretty much ready."

Sabah looked over her shoulder to Caron. The question was there in the little wrinkle between her eyebrows. They'd talked about just hiding in the backyard together but then neither of them had expected to be asked to help.

"I suppose," Caron said. "Though if it gets crowded we'll go hide in the back yard for a while."

"Totally fine," Duri said. "We've left the back yard alone, no decorations to scare anyone. But you will want to watch for slugs. They've come out to eat the fallen leaves. Still pretty out there, though."

She went on, chattering about how they'd rearranged the potted shrubs to create a little grotto in the back for cuddling. It was, apparently, going to be beautiful next year when the shrubs were fully leafed and the roses were in full bloom. Now it was cold and mildly damp. Not a place that sounded like fun. But maybe nice to retreat to when they needed a break.

Duri told them what to put where on the buffet table in the living room while Tiyamike buzzed around the kitchen pulling silverware, plates, glasses out of the cabinets. Yeah, Caron was going to want a break later. Tiyamike was heading towards overexposure quickly. She always got snappish when that happened, no matter how Duri tried to calm her down.

Sabah worked at Caron's side, setting everything perfectly squarely on the table. Which had an orange tablecloth with black jack-o-lanterns on it. New? Probably new. Caron hadn't seen it at last year's Halloween party.

The doorbell made her start and gasp.

"I got it!" Refilwe shouted as she ran down the stairs with Kaede at her heels.

Kaede had on a Little Bo Peep outfit that looked like it was designed for stage instead of fetish. The skirt came down past her knees, amazingly enough. They beamed as they gave a dozen little kids candy bars and praised their costumes. Caron blinked as Sabah touched her elbow.

"You."

"Like her?" Caron asked when Sabah didn't finish the statement but looked very hesitant. "No, I was wondering where she got a Little Bo Peep costume that had a knee-length skirt. I've only ever seen the miniskirt versions before."

Sabah blinked and then huffed a single little laugh that was utterly soundless but twice as heartfelt as any of Refilwe's booming belly laughs. She nodded and turned back to the buffet table. Caron caught her elbow and tugged her close for a hug and a kiss on the cheek that made Sabah stiffen.

"I like you best," Caron murmured. "Out of everyone, I like you best."

It was, apparently, the best thing she could have said. Sabah sighed and relaxed against her, hugging Caron hard enough that her ribs protested. They stood together like that until Duri chuckled and pushed them, gently, off to the side.

Which was fine because Kaede and Refilwe took over putting food out with Duri. Sabah smiled her microsecond smile, tugging at Caron's waist until she came along with her to sit next to Azar. Who nodded to them and changed the music to something soothing, uplifting, with a nice bouncy beat. Someday, maybe, Caron would learn the names of the songs Azar associated with her and Sabah. It wouldn't make sense to her but maybe Sabah could help interpret.

"I'm glad to see you, too, Azar," Caron said as she snuggled up next to Sabah, arms around Sabah's waist. "I like your costume."

"It works," Sabah said, nodding her agreement.

Azar didn't smile but she switched to the Addam's Family theme song and then to some of the old cheesy Halloween songs like Monster Mash so she was happy with the compliments. Caron's phone buzzed in her little purse. When she pulled it out there was a text that said 'U2' from Azar.

Caron smiled and sent back a thumb's up and a big smiley face. Maybe she'd manage to have a good Halloween tonight. At least with Sabah at her side she didn't have to worry about misinterpreting everything people said and did. That was nice.

Better than nice. Wonderful.

She set her head on Sabah's shoulder and sighed happily. Really. This was the best party ever. Sabah patted her hands before twisting around just enough that she could rub her cheek against Caron's.

Not a kiss but close. Caron blushed and smiled. Yeah. Definitely the best party ever. Sabah being there made a huge difference. But then she made a huge difference in Caron's life no matter what they were doing.

"Thank you," Caron whispered to Sabah. "I'm glad you're here."

"Me too," Sabah replied. "This. Feels better than I expected. Us. Not the party. Tiyamike's parties are always good."

"So true," Caron said. "She's great that way. I'm glad you're happy, too. Tell me if I do anything wrong, though."

"Always," Sabah promised. "But you don't usually. It's okay. I think the food is ready. Azar, did you want us to bring you a plate?"

Azar shook her head no, tucking her phone into her hoodie pocket. She nodded towards the buffet and signed 'come with me?'

"Yes," Caron said and signed back to her.

The three of them edged closer to the buffet, Caron worried about disturbing the others even though they weren't taking food. But then Duri spotted them and grinned as she pushed Tiyamike, Refilwe and Kaede off to the side, just as she had with Caron and Sabah. The three of them got food. Then so did Jun and Nkruma, Jun telling Nkruma what everything was and letting her choose what she wanted.

Eating on the couch was a little nervous-making but Sabah was there, too, calm and centered. She patted Caron's leg to reassure her. It was okay. Everything was okay.

Caron smiled and didn't start or spill her food when the front doorbell rang for more trick or treaters. Yeah. Best party yet.

THANKSGIVING

Leaves lay in lifeless drifts around Tiyamike's front steps. It wasn't too much of a surprise. Duri's sprained ankle meant that yard work was up to Tiyamike and she never stayed focused enough to finish it. That was why Duri always did it.

Caron bit her lip.

She really didn't want to be here. Yes, it was Thanksgiving. She always went to Tiyamike's Thanksgiving dinner. Caron certainly wasn't going to go visit her parents. Or her sister. That was a recipe for disaster. They scoffed at her, scolded her for taking her meds and gaslighted her every single time they talked. Adding a holiday when everyone was 'having fun' just made it worse.

Mom's idea of fun always seemed to involve talking about how much of a disappointment Caron was compared to her sister.

So Tiyamike's party was a better choice. Really. It was.

"Come on, kiddo," Refilwe said, gentle and kind as she rested a hand on Caron's shoulder. "You don't have to interact if you don't want to. It's good for you to get out of the house."

"I know," Caron said. Her eyes burned. "I just. Sabah."

Refilwe hugged her. "She'll be back, kiddo. You know she will."

Caron nodded even though she didn't know anything of the sort. Yes, Sabah had said that she'd be back but she'd taken all her clothes and her books when she went back home to visit her family. And that had been two weeks ago. There hadn't been a single phone call, text or email since then. No matter what Refilwe said, Caron didn't really believe that Sabah would be back.

It was over.

And Caron knew it.

She'd ruined another relationship. The best one she'd ever had. Sabah had been so wonderful to be around and now she was gone. Caron would never see her again. She'd spend the rest of her life alone, jumping at shadows, lost in the nightmares her stupid messed-up brain created.

"Inside, kiddo," Refilwe said. She tugged at Caron, pulling her up the path and stairs, just like that first visit at the housewarming party. "We'll tuck you in next to Azar. The two of you can spend some time texting to each other."

The instant the door opened, Tiyamike was there to hug Caron. A good solid hug, the sort that rocked you side to side. So Tiyamike had seen Caron break down outside. She had to be disgusted. Not that she looked it when she finally let Caron go.

"You mind helping Kaede for a minute?" Tiyamike asked. "The stereo's on the fritz so I need to steal Refilwe to fix it."

"Oh," Caron said, staring at Azar who was trembling as she stood next to the stereo, her phone clutched in her hands. "Um. Sure. Kitchen?"

"Yep," Tiyamike said. "I'm still not sure what Kaede's got

going on in there. She shoved us all out and said that we weren't allowed back in until it was time to serve. But I really think she needs an extra pair of hands. You're good at that."

Caron nodded. "You get too nervous. And Duri's ankle."

"Exactly," Tiyamike said. "Jun and Nkruma should be here in about half an hour. They're bringing pies."

Which explained why it needed to be Caron to help. Jun could help in the kitchen easily. Nkruma didn't mind having Jun do other things as long as she had someone to guide her around or a place to sit. And sitting with Azar while the stereo got fixed would be good. So Caron would help for a few minutes until Jun got there.

Then she'd go hide in the bathroom and cry for a while.

The kitchen smelled like turkey and sweet potatoes. There were three different pots cooking on the stove and six things in bowls that Caron couldn't immediately identify. Kaede turned towards her with a scowl that promised yelling but the moment she saw Caron the scowl turned into relief.

"Oh, thank goodness it's you," Kaede said. "Don't let them in. I swear, they're driving me up the wall. I need someone to mash the potatoes for me. I've got them ready, just haven't gotten them done. You just need to mash them."

"I can do that," Caron said. "Lumpy or really smooth?"

"Ah, I'd like lumpy but Azar's got a toothache on top of everything else so let's go for smooth," Kaede said. "Not milky, just not something that makes her chew too hard."

Caron nodded. She truly could do that. Might even help her feel better. Unlikely as that was. She put her coat over on the hooks at the back door, tied on Duri's apron, and then set to work mashing the potatoes until they were nicely squishy. They'd been cooking enough that they were soft, but not so much that they were liquid.

"You look sad," Kaede commented in a completely oblivious, what do I need to get done next tone of voice.

"Sabah left," Caron said. She stopped mashing. "She took all her things. Clothes. Shoes. Even her books. Everything. She left and went back home. It's been two weeks. I haven't heard anything. Not one word."

"Oh, baby," Kaede whispered. Her eyes were so sad when Caron risked a glance up at her. "I'm sorry. I thought she was coming back."

"I thought so too," Caron said. "She said she would. But then I haven't heard anything. Refilwe says she will. That she cares about me. I thought she did. But I haven't heard anything. So I don't know. It's hard. I'm really. Sad."

More than sad. Angry. Hurt. Afraid. Disappointed.

Her emotions where a churning mess that made no sense moment to moment. One bled into the other until they were as jumbled and squished up as the potatoes that Caron went back to mashing. Monday's session with her therapist had been pretty much nothing but Caron crying because she hadn't heard from Sabah. Her therapist had let her cry.

It hadn't really helped.

Crying. Sure, the tears eased things a little but the emotions were still there. Impossible to sort out and too big to handle.

The front door opened, closed. Caron sniffled, glad that Jun and Nkruma were there. She could go to the bathroom and hide for a while now. Except there wasn't any sound from the living room. No cheery greetings from Tiyamike. No laughter from Nkruma.

Just silence.

Both Kaede and Caron looked at the door, Kaede frowning. She set down her wooden spoon as Caron abandoned the mashed potatoes. But Caron didn't move more than a foot from the counter before Sabah appeared at the door.

She had a black eye. A split lip. Her hair had been roughly

chopped off, like someone had taken a knife to it or maybe kitchen shears, lopping off chunks while scolding Sabah.

Who stared and stared and stared at Caron, at the tears falling down Caron's face.

"Oh, my God," Kaede breathed. "Sabah, are you all right? Do you need to go to the hospital?"

"I'm fine," Sabah said, her tone as flat as always. "My family decided that I couldn't come back. That I wasn't queer. That my college classes didn't count. I got free. My grandfather is getting my things for me. They won't hurt him. He's old. I do need a new phone, though. My brother smashed mine."

Caron sobbed and ran to the bathroom. The little bathroom with it's cute pink curtains, purple shower curtain and fuzzy yellow toilet seat cover did nothing to calm Caron's tears. She heard Sabah's measured steps coming and dove into the bathtub, pulling the shower curtain to hide behind.

They'd hurt Sabah. It wasn't that Sabah didn't want Caron anymore. Her family had hurt her.

They'd hurt her!

How dare they hurt Sabah? It wasn't her fault that she couldn't express emotion the way everyone else did. She still had emotions. She had the right to go and live her life and do things her own way. Why would they hurt her and try to keep her from coming home?

Because it was home. The only home Caron had anymore was with Sabah by her side. Refilwe was there, yes, but it wasn't the same with just her. Sabah made everything better. So much better.

The bathroom door opened. Closed. The lock clicked shut.

"I'm sorry," Sabah said. It sounded like she was sitting on the toilet.

"Sorry," Caron said.

Sobbed. She buried her face in her knees, rocking as she tried to get her emotions back under control. Somehow.

"Are you angry at me?" Sabah asked. There was a hint of worry. Fear.

"No!" Caron huffed. "Not you. Them. Me. The world. Too many emotions. Too much. I can't. It's all. A mess. Jumbled. My head is, is, is mashed potatoes, squished up nonsense. I don't. Damn it."

"Oh," Sabah said and this time there was definitely relief in her voice, faint as it was. "Okay then. You can cry if you want. We can go upstairs, sit in the office. It's more comfortable than the bathtub. I'm tired. Grandma saved my car for me. I drove back, all in one day. Ten hours. I didn't want to be away any longer than I had to. I missed you. And everyone else but mostly you."

Caron's eyes burned with tears as she sobbed and laughed and pulled the edge of the shower curtain back so that she could peek at Sabah. Whose lips twitched in a little smile before smoothing back out to normal.

Other than the split lip. It looked really painful. So did her black eye. That eye was completely swollen shut.

"You need an ice pack for your face," Caron said as she rubbed the tears off her cheeks with her sleeve.

"You need to blow your nose," Sabah said, nodding her agreement. "Upstairs? I think I need some hugs."

"As many hugs as you want," Caron promised. "Just with the ice pack on your face."

She scrambled back out of the tub, surprised with herself. Normally she'd have stayed right there for hours, until someone needed to go pee. But with Sabah sitting there, obviously hurting, Caron found it amazingly easy to get up. To take Sabah's hand. The knuckles were bruised. She'd punched someone.

"They deserved it," Caron said, staring at Sabah's black and blue knuckles. "I hope you hurt them. A lot."

"A little," Sabah said with her microsecond smile. "Grandpa says that he's going to press charges for me. So it won't happen again. After he gets my things back. They probably think I'm still in the state, hiding at Grandma and Grandpa's. I wouldn't though. I wanted to come home."

She stared at Caron as she said 'home'. Caron blushed and tried not to burst in to tears again. Stupid emotions. She needed to stop that. At least until Sabah had an ice pack for her face. Then they'd go upstairs and cuddle and hide until dinner was done.

"It's home when you're here," Caron said. "Not so much when you're gone."

"Then I won't go away again," Sabah promised so instantly that Caron blushed and fought another sob. "Come on. Let's go sit together. I need hugs."

Caron nodded. Thanksgiving was. Well. Not going to be as bad as she'd thought. Not now that Sabah was back. It might even be good, sort of.

CHRISTMAS

Caron stood next to her new car, staring at Tiyamike's house. There were lights. Lots of lights. Multicolored, draped across the roof and dangling from the gutters. They'd put lights in the windows and along the path and through every single picket on their fence. The shrubs, so neatly trimmed that they were perfect squares, were covered with nets of lights that cheerfully blinked at Caron.

Sabah slowly climbed out of the car, their contribution of sticky buns held in her arms. "That's a lot of lights."

"I wasn't entirely sure I wasn't hallucinating," Caron admitted. "How much are they spending on electricity this month?"

When Sabah glanced her way, there was laughter in her eyes. And a tiny quirk of a smile on her lips. If Sabah had been anyone else, she would have burst out laughing. Caron didn't need the laugh. The little smile said even more as far as Caron was concerned.

"Too much," Sabah said. "Let's head inside. It's wet."

It was. The rain had held off most of the day. But now it was drizzling down, not so hard as to make Caron run for the front door but hard enough that her shoes were wet and her shoulders getting thoroughly soaked by the time they walked up the path.

Where Duri appeared, towels in hand. She grinned at them, nodding so that the sparkly red antlers with their flashing lights would bob on her head. Caron squeaked and then laughed because Duri laughed with delight at the expression on Caron's face.

"Those are hideous," Sabah said with just enough awe in her voice that it made Duri strike a pose.

"Aren't they?" Duri said. She waved for them to come in. "We've got gifts going under the tree and food into the kitchen. Watch out, Refilwe and Kaede teamed up with Azar to create something really stupendous for dinner. Not sure what it is but it smells amazing."

It really did. Caron sniffed as they left their wet shoes and coats by the front door. Her bag with the little five dollar gifts they'd all agreed on went under the tree. The sticky buns went into Tiyamike's arms. She was wearing eight necklaces of tiny Christmas lights around her neck and she had little snowmen that lit up randomly dangling like earrings from her ears.

"So glad you two made it!" Tiyamike said, hugging them both once the sticky buns were tucked into the one clear spot on the counter over by the toaster. "You guys get the boxes unpacked?"

"We did," Sabah said. "There's still one box with toilet paper but our new apartment is set up."

That was the biggest change they'd had since Thanksgiving. Well, one of the big changes. Caron had gotten to meet Sabah's grandmother and grandfather. They were very nice people, sweet and loving. Both of them adored Sabah and couldn't be happier that she'd found someone who accepted her just as she was.

Apparently, Sabah's parents and brother were still insisting that Sabah would be 'just fine', 'normal' if she'd get married to a man and let him have sex with her. Horrible people. Sabah and her grandparents were suing them for assault, battery, kidnapping, emotional abuse, torture, attempted sexual assault, sex trafficking (because none of them cared that Sabah had repeatedly said no to the man who'd been chosen to 'fix' her by raping her) and about six other charges related to them trying to steal Sabah's trust fund and wages.

It wasn't safe for Sabah to stay in her old apartment so she'd broken the lease and gotten a new one in a much nicer place with Caron.

So now they were roommates as well as dating and Caron was surprised at how easy that was. Sex was definitely not on the agenda, not after what Sabah had gone through, but frankly Caron wasn't sure she wanted that sort of thing anyway. Their relationship was so completely practical, friends that cuddled and shared everything together, that it didn't bother Caron.

"Everything's working out?" Tiyamike said, looking more at Caron than at Sabah.

"Oh yes," Caron said. "Sabah's so practical about everything that it doesn't really feel like a romance. Just. Well. Friends who decided to spend their lives together, I guess. That's fine."

"And the sex isn't an issue with Caron so I'm happy," Sabah said so firmly that Tiyamike's face bloomed into a smile.

"Good," Tiyamike said. "Probably best to get out of the kitchen. Refilwe and Kaede are on a roll with Azar. She's apparently decided cooking is a thing she likes, as long as someone else mixes all the ingredients and touches the food for her."

"Texting them the instructions?" Sabah asked.

Tiyamike nodded. From what Caron could see, looking past her shoulder, Refilwe and Kaede were having a blast with it. Azar was even smiling as she stood next to them, fingers flying on her phone screen as she texted them what to do. It seemed a little weird but this was the sort of thing that Kaede adored, figuring out a new recipe, and Refilwe loved any chance to interact with people doing things they enjoyed.

"They're doing well together?" Caron asked Tiyamike. "I felt bad about leaving Refilwe with the whole lease."

Tiyamike snorted and gently shooed them out of the kitchen and into the living room where Duri was furtively shaking presents to see if she could figure out what they were. Duri went beet red and tried to thrust the package back under the tree as if they hadn't seen her playing with it already.

"They're doing great," Tiyamike said. She huffed at Duri, hands on her hips, snorting when Duri tried to look extra innocent and batted her eyes. "Kaede's really glad to have someone with energy around. She has a hard time in the mornings. And Refilwe said that she's delighted to have someone with such a high paycheck living with her. Kaede's job is just..."

Tiyamike waved her hands in the air, rolling her eyes. Which, yes. Kaede's software job was well beyond Caron's understanding but she knew that it paid far better than anyone else's in their group. Kaede was always glad to help out when someone was short.

Sabah caught Caron's hand, pulling her towards the stairs and Duri and Tiyamike stared at each other in that 'about to have a not-fight flirting session' way that Caron always found disturbing despite knowing that it wasn't serious.

They slipped upstairs to the office, curling up on the love seat together.

"I'm glad," Caron murmured as she cuddled Sabah.

There was still a flinch when Caron hugged Sabah but she relaxed much faster now than she had at Thanksgiving. Every day she got better and better. Maybe in a few years she wouldn't twitch at all when Caron hugged her or touched her cheek. Poor Sabah. Her cheek still hurt. The bone had been fractured, not that Sabah had admitted it until almost two weeks after she escaped from her family.

"That Refilwe is okay?" Sabah asked.

"Yes."

"She would be," Sabah said, rubbing Caron's back gently. Her hand was warm and broad, a comforting counterpoint to the smell of roasting beef, spices and pine trees that filled the air. "Refilwe is strong. Very little stops her."

"I know," Caron agreed. "But she doesn't admit that she needs help sometimes. Not until things go poorly. Kaede will do a good job keeping that from happening, I think."

Sabah nodded. "She will. Like I do for you."

"And I do for you," Caron said, grinning as Sabah's cheeks went red.

The office was quiet. Comforting. Outside, the rain stepped up from drizzle to a pounding downpour that rattled against the roof. It got louder and louder until Caron looked out the window. Sleet. No, hail. It was a hail storm.

"I thought the weather said it would be too cold for that," Caron said. The office did seem colder than it should be.

"I guess they were wrong," Sabah said. She stared out the window, too, watching with Caron as the hail grew in size, then shrank again, then turned into drifting flakes of snow that melted the instant they touched anything.

"The drive home is going to be horrible," Caron

commented a few minutes later. "It's going to get colder overnight."

"Mm-hmm," Sabah said. She frowned. "Jun and Nkruma aren't here yet."

They exchanged a worried look and then went downstairs to find Azar at her phone in the living room, texting someone. Not anyone else because they were all clustered around the TV listening to the weather report. Which was now talking about a cold snap sweeping down from the north to engulf the Puget Sound in surprise winter weather for Christmas.

"Jun and Nkruma are staying home?" Caron asked Azar.

She shook her head no, signing 'telling to' at Caron.

"Good idea," Caron agreed. "If it gets any colder the roads are going to be solid ice."

"We're not going to be able to get up the hill into our duplex," Sabah said. "Not until mid-morning tomorrow anyway."

"Doesn't matter," Tiyamike declared. She put her hands on her hips and glared at the snow slowly drifting down outside. "You guys can spend the night. We'll up out the air mattress, get all our extra blankets, make a sleepover of it. I mean, if you've all got your meds with you?"

Which, Caron blinked, she wasn't sure. But when she turned to Sabah, Sabah nodded confidently, smiling her microsecond smile at Caron. Alex snorted and flapped one hand at Tiyamike while Kaede pulled a little bag full of pills out of her pocket.

"Dude, I use the same meds at the same dose that you do," Refilwe said to Tiyamike. "If Kaede didn't have me covered, you would. I'm fine. Though honestly, Kaede and I could probably make it home no problem. Our place is on a major street that's really well salted and plowed during snow events."

Snow event.

Caron turned to the window again, delight starting to bubble up. They were having a snow even. On Christmas Eve.

"There's going to be a white Christmas," Caron said, starting to laugh as she took Sabah's hand. "We're getting a white Christmas, Sabah. Our first Christmas together."

Sabah's eyes went wide. Azar stopped texting, turning to stare at Caron with her mouth open. She blinked about a thousand times as she processed that. Then Azar started giggling as she went back to texting Jun and Nkruma.

Refilwe hooted, cheering as she grabbed Caron and Sabah for a hug that was as bouncy as it was boisterous. Behind her, Kaede started singing White Christmas while Tiyamike beamed at them both.

"We never get a white Christmas around here," Refilwe exclaimed. "Dude, we need to make, like hot chocolate and sugar cookies tomorrow morning. I mean, the snow probably won't last that long tomorrow. But we should still do it. I mean, come on."

"With as many leftovers as we'll have?" Tiyamike said only to groan as even Azar turned puppy eyes on her. "Oh. My. God! Fine, hot chocolate and cookies tomorrow. Duri, do we have that sugar cookie dough in the freezer still."

"Oh yeah," Duri said as she headed for the kitchen. "We got like three dozen cookies worth. And I know we've got powdered sugar. We can make some simple frosting for them. I think we've got food color tucked away somewhere. This is going to be awesome!"

Christmas carols started playing over the stereo as Caron's phone buzzed in her pocket. When she pulled it out, there was a text from Azar saying 'Merry Christmas!' Caron grinned at her, showed Sabah and then laughed as Sabah tugged her close for a hug. The first one Sabah had initiated since she escaped from her family.

"I like this family," Sabah whispered to Caron.

"Mmm, they're good, aren't they?" Caron said. "I mean, we're all broken, sort of, but we try. We work well together."

"No, we're only broken around other people," Sabah said. "Here, together, we're not broken at all. We're just right."

Caron blinked at her and then laughed as she tucked her face into the nook of Sabah's neck. She nodded and Sabah hummed softly while rubbing Caron's back. Yes. This was right. Even though Sabah's silver sweater, soft and fuzzy in the extreme, tickled her nose, this was perfect.

"I'm glad I came to Tiyamike's housewarming," Sabah murmured.

"Me, too," Caron replied. "So glad. Come on. Let's cuddle next to Azar. This is home. Our home. And our family, the one that we chose and they chose us. It's good."

"It's better than that," Sabah agreed. They settled next to Azar who smiled just for a second before playing I'll be Home for Christmas for them. "It's perfect."

Caron couldn't disagree with that. She snuggled with Sabah and listened to the music. The chill from the cold wave couldn't penetrate Tiyamike's house. Not with all the love and the good food and the laughter coming from the kitchen as Tiyamike and Duri bickered happily about which cookie cutters to use while Kaede and Refilwe fussed over the dish they were making for Azar.

Home. The old saying was right. This was where Caron's heart was so yes, it was home. And she'd never let them go, all of them. Her family, broken and perfect, every single one of them.

"Merry Christmas," Caron whispered to Sabah.

"Merry Christmas," Sabah whispered back, kissing Caron's temple. "Merry Christmas to us all."

AUTHOR'S NOTE: THE ABSENCE OF WRATH

We move on to something just a bit spooky, just a bit off kilter from the world we all know. Manu knows all about being off from the people around him. Not white enough, not straight enough, and sure as hell not rich enough, he's always on guard.

Until a midnight trudge through the rain gifts him with something he could never have imagined and something that he might just want to accept.

THE ABSENCE OF WRATH

Rain dripped down Manu's nose, curling under the tip to puddle on his upper lip. He licked the latest drop off without stopping his slow trudge. A car whooshed by him, spraying mud and water across the sidewalk to splatter against his thigh. Again.

If he'd brought an umbrella. A hat. Jacket with a hood. Any of those would made this whole walk of shame less irritating. But, of course, he'd left everything sensible at home because there was no way that Kapua would flake out on him.

Again.

Should've learned the last time he had to walk three miles home from one of those stupid parties Kapua was always dragging him off to. Only bright spot was that his pants, muddy and soaked though they were, had reflective panels.

He wouldn't get run over tonight. Probably.

Rain battered down around him, shattering on the sidewalk and splashing in the puddles where fallen leaves had filled the drains. Another car flew by, spraying more muddy water. Manu didn't flinch from it as it drenched him in ice.

No point. He was so wet that it wouldn't make a bit of difference.

Another car, slower this time, drove closer, then slowed. It stopped next to Manu, the window slowly going down in an electric hum.

Okay, huh. A way for the night to get even worse. Manu hadn't expected that.

He stiffened until a big black guy switched on the cab light and peered across the passenger seat at him. Nice face, full lips that looked bitten up and dry, but he was clean, well-dressed in a suit and loosened tie. And his eyes were full of nothing but worry for Manu.

"Hey, man, you need a ride?" the guy asked.

"I'm almost home," Manu said even though he really, seriously wasn't. "Thanks, though."

"You sure?" the guy asked with a frown at the road. No, at his radio. "Dude, there's reports of some sort of stalker with a weapon on the loose or something. Just up the road in this area. Cops got called to a party a mile or so from here. Not a good night to be out and about."

"Uh."

Fucking Kapua. Manu should've dragged his ass out…

"That's… not good," Manu said. "I mean, wait. Why aren't you worried it's me?"

"Because they say he has a car?" the guy said, blinking at Manu as if that was the strangest question in the world to ask. "Flashy red thing with a jacked-up engine."

Fucking Kapua!

"I… don't have a car," Manu said in leu of anything sensible.

"Yeah, exactly," the guy said. "Look, it's cool. I can take you close to home, drop you off. I got a rain coat you can sit on if you're worried about the seat. It's just not safe out here tonight."

Manu grimaced but nodded. Didn't look like the guy was going to give and anyone else would've already said yes. Took just a minute for the guy to spread out his raincoat, nice pricey one that would actually keep rain off, over the seat. Manu settled into the seat and shut the door, dripping everywhere but trying to confine it to his seat.

"Thanks," Manu said as the guy headed up the road again at a perfectly on-the-dot speed. "Friend of mine ditched me at a party so I was walking home. Should've brought a hat or something."

"Yeah, definitely," the guy said with a wry little smile at Manu. "You're sopping, man. Where'm I taking you?"

Manu considered it for a moment.

Logic said he should head home but with Kapua apparently on a tear, home wasn't a good place to be. And if Kapua really was wanted by the cops, that apartment was not a great place to be anyway. Manu should go home-home but no way was he going back to his parents. That left crashing on Kai's couch. At least Kai was close and he'd given Manu one of the keys and said anything he needed to crash away from Kapua it was fine.

So, Manu shrugged. "Turn onto Mukilteo Drive. I'm crashing with a friend in one of the big complexes near the high school."

The guy nodded but the worried frown was back. A fretter, great. At least with the cab light off, there was little chance of the guy having a good look at Manu. And, between the mud and water, he didn't look much like his normal self anyway.

Though why Manu would be worried about a complete stranger outing him to his parents, Manu didn't know. Habit, probably. Didn't seem like that bad of a guy, if a bit ridiculous about helping complete strangers who could kill him or something.

"I'm Ekene," the guy said after they turned into Mukilteo Drive and began the slow twenty mile an hour crawl down it's winding path along the Mukilteo cliffs.

"Manu."

"So, against my better judgement," Ekene said with a little glance sideways at Manu, "I'm asking. Why were you walking in the rain in the middle of the night in nothing but a T-shirt and some flashy pants?"

"Went to a party," Manu said with a dripping shrug, "realized it wasn't my scene, like, at all, and then decided to hoof it home when my friend flaked out on me. Again. He's a jerk. Not doing that again."

Ekene snorted a laugh. "Okay, that's better than I was expecting."

"Do not want to know what you thought I was doing," Manu said. He held up his hands and whoa, the fingernails were blue in the light of a passing streetlamp. "Nope. Not interested. Not going there."

Ekene laughed for real, a good deep laugh that filled the car with warmth. "Probably for the best. Which one am I heading for again?"

Manu pointed the way, which wasn't hard. Mukilteo Drive went right past the place but once they pulled in, Ekene stopping his car right in front of Kai's place, Manu froze. Kai's parents' truck was there. His very homophobic, very judgmental, very prone to lectures and beatings parents. All the lights were still on even though it was way late for Kai to be up.

"Well, fuck."

"Problem?" Ekene asked with enough worry that Manu frowned at him.

"Why do you care?" Manu asked. "You don't know me."

"You're already dripping on my car, man," Ekene said with a sort of embarrassed look. No way to tell if he blushed in this light but man, Manu was pretty sure his cheeks were hot from the way Ekene's shoulders hunched and his fingers clenched on the steering wheel. "I mean, I made the offer to get you home safe and if there's a problem, well, that's a problem for me."

"Do-gooder," Manu muttered only to laugh in spite of himself when Ekene groaned and thumped his forehead against the steering wheel. "Oh, serious do-gooder, huh? You often rescue people this way?"

"Not really," Ekene grumbled but there was no heat to it. "I mean, yeah, but not like this. More like giving someone a twenty when I see them panhandling or donating to shelters and things. I just. It's raining and you were walking with no coat or anything. It got to me."

Manu raised an eyebrow while considering what to do next. Home was still out. He didn't have any friends close other than Kai and Kapua. More questions.

"Been there?" Manu asked, not really believing it could be so.

"...Yeah," Ekene said after a long enough pause that Manu frowned at him. "I have. Not since I was really young but yes. I have. Not just out in the rain but stuck with an abusive asshole controlling my life and no way out other than taking a blind-stupid chance. It worked out for me. I. I try to help where I can when I see someone who's in the same sort of bind."

There was something about the way Ekene said it that raised the soggy hair on the back of Manu's neck. This was not just bad parents and bad lover territory. Ekene's fingers were so tight on the steering wheel that it creaked. For a second his eyes flashed like a dog's in the darkness of the car, lit by the headlights of a passing cop car.

Patrolling cops. Yeah, Kapua really had fucked up this time. Sure, the cops always patrolled this neighborhood. All the big apartment complexes pulled in the crazies and the hand-to-mouth-ers. Made for more crime.

And more brown people who didn't dare fight back when the cops decided that they were up to trouble, even if they weren't.

Both Manu and Ekene froze as the cop car turned into the apartment complex.

"Staying or going?" Ekene asked.

"Drive," Manu replied.

Ekene drove. Sedately, perfectly on the speed limit. Out of the apartment complex with the cop car on their ass. Then up Mukilteo Drive, left on the Speedway heading north towards the docks, only to turn right to head along the Boeing Freeway. He kept right on driving, taking the two of them north out of Everett.

"I expected more questions about where we're going," Ekene asked once they were on I5 heading north.

"I am officially out of places to crash," Manu admitted. "I mean, I got other friends but they all need notice before I drop on them. Kai, where I wanted you to drop me, would take me in anytime. But his parents are there and they're assholes. And Kapua?"

Manu shook his head and then snorted a laugh as Ekene glanced at him all worried and protective. That was cute. Not like Manu couldn't protect himself. He'd been couch surfing long enough that he knew how to take care of himself. Sure, he'd need to make a dash home to get more clothes if the cops seized everything in Kapua's place but he could survive that when it came.

"Kapua?" Ekene asked, steering wheel creaking again. He was seriously strong, something to remember, though Ekene did loosen his fingers abruptly when Manu glanced his way.

"Kapua's probably who the cops are searching for," Manu

said. "Part of what I meant about that party not being my scene at all."

Ekene groaned and shook his head. He didn't speed up as he drove them north to Marysville, then onwards to Arlington. The new big shopping centers around Arlington would've been where Manu'd have pegged Ekene to live but he turned right, east, not west. They went past the Arlington excuse of an airport with its grass runway and then up the hill into a suburban development area with big four and five bedroom places that probably sold at half a million a pop.

Okay, so Ekene was doing even better than Manu thought. There was serious money up here. Farms on the south side of the road. Huge houses on the north. Then Ekene threw Manu for a loop by heading even further out of town into the true boonies between Arlington and Granite Falls.

"I give," Manu said once they passed the roundabout that led either south to Granite Falls, north to old Arlington, or straight east into the hills. They went east. "Where're we going, man?"

Ekene laughed, his teeth flashing in the night like fangs except it was a real welcoming smile. "I have some land out this way. Twenty acres. I've got my house there. It's a bitch of drive into Seattle but most of the time I work remote. My boss doesn't care if I'm in the office every day or not. You're lucky that I was out today. Most of the time I don't bother going anywhere if I don't have to."

"Nice gig," Manu said because yeah, that would be nice. Work from home and still get paid. He wished. Hard.

"It is," Ekene agreed. "Just makes home not feel like home after a while. You never get away from work when it's right there in your face twenty-four seven."

Manu nodded thoughtfully as he watched the wet, dark woods illuminated in Ekene's headlights. Not a house or streetlight around. Hard as hell to get out of here if this was a bad choice but it was actually a bit too late to fuss over that. Like half an hour, forty minutes too late.

They turned onto a narrow gravel road, well-tended with only a few potholes in it. That went on for, like, forever. At least ten minutes. Then they were suddenly there, at Ekene's house. Which was maybe three bedrooms, nice old-fashioned looking two-story rustic place with cedar shake all over the walls and roof, big porch and a carport that had a big pickup sitting next to an empty spot.

"Nice car for work, real truck for the rest of the time," Manu commented, more than a little amused by the old truck compared to the flashy car and Ekene's nice suit.

Ekene laughed and shrugged. "You gotta have a truck out here. Can't tell you how many times I've had to use the truck to pull logs off the lane. Come on. Let's head inside and get you cleaned up. I've got some food in the fridge, too. I ate in Seattle but if you're hungry, feel free."

The rain'd eased up a lot out here, down to a slow sprinkle that was barely even noticeable to Manu after a lifetime of Puget Sound rainstorms. All around the carport and house, though, there were looming cedar trees and huge old maple and elm. The rain dripping off them wasn't fine, misty rain. It was big, fat drops that hit the back of Manu's neck like icy grenades.

He followed Ekene into the house, stopping in his tracks once Ekene flicked the lights on.

Dude had money with a capital M. Big damn couch with nice leather, all new-looking. The pristine wood floor had real oriental carpets on it, for walking on even. Big oil paintings on the wall. All of them with a nice African theme to them which was way better than the stupid English Garden paintings you usually say in rich people's houses.

The living room was open right up to the roof, big and

airy and warm somehow despite the openness. Huge fireplace covered with rock had a woodstove instead of an open hearth. And the kitchen was the size of Kapua's whole apartment, all shiny stainless steel with polished wood counters.

"Bathroom's off to the right," Ekene said as he hung up the expensive raincoat by the door. "Just kick your shoes off and head on in. I'll bring you some clothes, start heating up the leftovers in the fridge."

"Man, I really can't say thank you enough," Manu said because what the hell else could he say?

This could go wrong so many ways and he really didn't know why it hadn't yet. Manu was dressed in the finest 'I might be a hooker and I might not, why don't you ask' that he could manage. Rich dude picking up a maybe-hooker on the side of the road at night? Perfect recipe for Manu disappearing in the woods forever. Not like anyone had the faintest clue where he was. Manu hadn't even bothered to call someone before taking this ride.

He toed off his shoes, squelched into the bathroom which was sleek and modern but with warm wood paneling instead of chrome and glass everywhere. Nice shower that Manu looked forward to spending far too much time in.

No TP under the sink, just the one roll on the holder. No tweezers or lube or athlete's foot stuff in the cabinet. Not even a single cotton swab tucked away. Hell, there wasn't a single toothbrush in the whole bathroom. Manu bit his lip and considered it again as his heart pounded like he was running a marathon.

"Got some sweats for you," Ekene said.

He knocked once on the door and then thrust them into the bathroom at Manu. Looked so damned nervous that Manu caught his wrist to keep him from running away. There was that flash in his eyes, like there was a mirror at the back of his eyeballs instead of blood vessels.

Ekene's skin was cold as ice.

Manu licked his lips, tasting sweat, mud, rain, fear. This. This.

Not what he'd thought, then. Manu nodded, squeezing Ekene's wrist which didn't have a pulse at all under that dark brown skin. No pulse, no warmth, weird eyes. Yeah, not what Manu'd been assuming at all.

Especially given that Ekene got more and more tense as the seconds ticked by, his expression going from uncomfortable to outright panicky.

"Dude," Manu said so shakily that he laughed, shook his head and tried again. "Seriously, you have got to be more careful about the people you bring home. I could be, like, a thief or a serial killer or something."

He let go of Ekene's wrist so that he could take the clothes. Nice new sweats, good and thick that would keep him warm easily. Ekene blew out a breath as he rubbed his wrist where Manu'd held him. Weird part was that Ekene looked more uncomfortable than Manu did with the whole thing.

Been there. That's what he'd said. He'd been trapped and escaped and now he tried to help where he could. And he lived out in the middle of nowhere, had a job that let him not interact with people except when he wanted to. Good gig. Plenty of money. House like a magazine spread instead of a real home.

"I should be saying that to you," Ekene countered with a wry little smile that showed his teeth for only a fraction of a second. They were very white. No chance to see if any were pointed.

"You are not saying anything I haven't already thought about sixty million times tonight," Manu declared as he tossed the clothes on the counter. "And that was before I got in your car. Want me to toss the clothes on the floor or pass 'em out to you? I'm assuming you think they might just possibly need a little bit of a wash."

Ekene burst out laughing. Hard enough that Manu grinned at him. Oh yeah, he knew that laugh. The 'thank fuck they let that go, I'm safe' laugh. Not the same reason that Manu gave that laugh but he knew the feeling behind it. And understood the relief on Ekene's face when he shrugged and gestured at Manu's muddy pants.

"You gotta admit they're trashed," Ekene said.

"That they are," Manu agreed. "Floor?"

"Floor works," Ekene said. "I'll set up a place for you to sleep on the couch. Tomorrow, later today, really, we'll see about finding you a place to crash. Or taking you back to your friend's place if his parents are gone."

"That works," Manu said.

He flipped his fingers at Ekene, snickering as Ekene made elaborate haste to shut the door. Ekene's laughter, deep and relieved, danced under the door. Manu sagged a little and then shook his head at himself. He still had rain dripping down his hair, off his nose.

Time to get cleaned up. Then he'd see where things went next. Who knew? Maybe it'd be somewhere better than Manu'd been heading in life. It worked for Ekene. A second chance might work for him, too.

AUTHOR'S NOTE: DANDELION INTRIGUES

This one is based on the college I went to, with events that I personally lived through. The storm was a bomb cyclone that hit my university and my dorm room windows froze up just like Ellington's. I wasn't so lucky as to get to date a gorgeous man out of it, but that's okay. I also wasn't so optimistic as to walk across campus in shorts in the middle of winter.

DANDELION INTRIGUES

*E*llington whistled along with the birds as he strolled across the University of Montana quad in shorts for the first time of the year. The sun was finally out, battling the nose-nipping breeze to warm his legs and back as he walked. After a winter that had included a school-shutting storm with minus ninety windchill outside, the sun was a blessing.

He'd never been that cold and that sweaty just from walking inside and climbing the stairs up to his third-floor dorm room. So cold that his nose hair had frozen as he tried to breathe the ice-crystal-filled air, only to walk into a sauna in his room. Everyone in the basement had cranked their heaters to the max so that they wouldn't freeze. All that heat had one place to go: straight up to Ellington's room where the windows had frozen shut.

The storm had finally passed. Even if there were still snowbanks scattered everywhere, they were melting fast enough that Ellington had declared spring. So what if his legs had goosebumps and his fingernails were going blue? It wasn't that far from his dorm to the library. Spring was finally here and damn it, he was going to enjoy it.

The grass, once brown, had gone bright and green as fresh new shoots pushed up through last year's turf. Dandelions had started to wage their endless war for victory against the groundskeepers at the same time so Ellington could see beautiful dots of yellow everywhere across the quad. He should go gather leaves and add them to a salad. Grandma would've yelled at him for wasting good nutrients by walking by spring dandelions.

Overhead, the single-file line of imported elms were just beginning to show buds. For now their black branches rattled against each other in the wind, bare as if winter was still in full swing. That didn't bother the singing birds at all. Most of the trees around the long oval of the quad were pines with plenty of shelter for birds to build snug little nests.

Ellington's teeth chattered abruptly.

Okay, so maybe it was still too cold for shorts.

He looked around and then broke into a shuffling jog. Not much faster but it made him look more like he wasn't crazy. Just exercising. With his backpack. Full of books. On his way to the library. Yeah. That's all. It was training for… something.

Ellington shuffle-jogged past two coeds wearing parkas who stared at him as if he'd lost his mind. Eyes forward, nothing to see here. Nope, just training. Yep, that was it, training for oh, not a marathon. That was way too long. A half-marathon? Hell, he was training to get in shape after the long, cold winter. That was it.

Before Ellington's lungs could explode, he exited the quad, passed the University bookstore and wobbled into the glass double doors of the library. Okay, not doing that again. His legs shook so hard he wasn't sure he was going to be able to climb the stairs. Sweat was already dripping down his back and man, breathing while jogging was outright impossible.

"Oh, hey, saw you out jogging," Leslie Pherigo said behind Ellington. "You taking up running?"

Leslie Pherigo of the broad shoulders, the warm blue eyes, the smell of baby powder and smiles that melted away every bit of the chill that'd settled into Ellington. Or maybe that was his blush which roared through him like a dragon intent on burning every inch of his skin until he was beet red.

"Uh, kinda," Ellington said. "Long winter, you know? It'd be good to get back in shape."

"God, don't I know it," Leslie groaned. He patted his rock-hard stomach. "I swear I've put on a good ten pounds."

"Where?" Ellington asked only to discover that no, yeah, he could totally blush harder.

Leslie laughed, patting Ellington's shoulder. "Thank you for stoking my ego. I seriously need it. Study session for Physics?"

"Oh, no, I've got a tutoring thing I'm doing," Ellington said. At least standing here embarrassing himself had gotten his heart to slow down enough that he didn't feel like it was going to go straight through his chest. "Charley asked me to help him with English 101. He's struggling and, you know, spare cash is always nice."

"Oh, my god," Leslie breathed while staring at Ellington like he was God, Jesus and Moses all wraped up in an American flag, complete with an eagle riding his shoulder. "I didn't know you did tutoring on English? I'm really struggling with my Lit class. Could I get a session with you?"

Huh. Well. Hearts could try to tear themselves out of your chest without running. Who knew?

"Uh, sure?" Ellington said. His voice came out squeaky as his mom's lap dog's rubber duckie so Ellington cleared his throat and tried again. "Yeah, sure, that's fine. Um, when's it due?"

"Not for two weeks," Leslie said, still with stars in his eyes. "Can we meet up, say, after dinner? Or we could meet at the cafeteria, eat and then come here?"

Ellington tried to say yes but nothing came out. He nodded while making garbled squeaking noises that were going to haunt him until the day he died. It didn't seem to matter to Leslie who beamed and clapped Ellington's shoulder hard enough to stagger Ellington.

"Thank you so much!" Leslie exclaimed. "I've got to go do my physics study session. Meet you at the north door to the cafeteria at five? Six?"

"M-make it six," Ellington said.

"It's a date!" Leslie said, waving and running up the stairs like the hunk of American godhood made flesh that he was.

Ellington stood there, gaping, for a good minute and a half before one of the librarians wandered over and asked if he was okay. He still could only make squeaky rubber duckie noises. She laughed as Ellington escaped up the stairs to his tutoring session. Which probably went well? Charley seemed to understand what Ellington said, not that Ellington had the slightest clue what they'd looked at, what he'd said or anything.

A date.

He had a sort-of date with Leslie Pherigo. Except, no, probably not really. Missoula, Montana wasn't as bad as some places. It wasn't like backwoods in the deep south. Or, hell, backwoods Montana, for that matter. Ellington wasn't going to get beaten up for liking a guy here. Maybe.

He'd definitely gotten beaten up for being a complete failure at everything sports-related and for being shorter than most girls and for being too much of a brain with not enough sense to get out of a wet paper bag in the rain, as his mom always said.

But not for being gay, thankfully.

Yet.

Leslie was too gorgeous a guy. He had girls hanging off him all the time. Where Ellington was a nobody with a probable good career in some boring office job ahead of him, Leslie was sure to be way more successful. Just a fact. He was the sort of guy who would go far, do great things, see the world. All that jazz.

None of which included having a boyfriend who couldn't shuffle-jog his way across one quarter of the quad, like less than two blocks. Heck, no way was Leslie looking for a boyfriend at all. Not a guy like that.

Having done... something... satisfactory enough to help Charley figure out his English 101 assignment and having argued himself back into a semi-sane state of mind, Ellington headed out of the library and immediately began fast shuffle-jogging his way back across the quad to his dorm.

Damn but it got cold over the last couple of hours!

Ellington hauled his sweaty, frozen carcass into the showers, got cleaned up, and then put on real clothes and a coat to head to dinner.

To his date.

Oh, God. He was doomed. Ellington had a date with Leslie who stood outside the doors of the cafeteria in a perfect blue peacoat that hugged his body like a glove. His slacks were charcoal and his smile warmed Ellington straight through as soon as he spotted Ellington hurrying his way.

"You're right on time," Leslie said. "Come on. It's gotten colder. I thought we were going to have spring earlier."

"No kidding," Ellington agreed. "The sunshine fooled me into wearing shorts."

"Fooled or not, they looked good on you," Leslie said.

Ellington stared at him.

"No, really," Leslie said as he passed over his meal pass to the gal behind the register, then took it back without looking. "You did. I mean, you've got actual calves. I've got chicken legs. No matter how hard I work out, they're still skinny."

"He's crazy," Ellington said to the easily seventy-year-old gal on the register as he passed over his meal pass.

"I think he wears his chicken legs well," the gal said, grinning at the two of them. "Better hurry. They had a nice roast just coming out of the oven a minute or two ago. Enjoy your dinner, boys."

Roast beast and mashed potatoes with scads of butter and sour cream, fresh warm rolls with real butter and cherry pie with ice cream made for an awesome dinner. Leslie added a salad with blue cheese dressing, so much of it that it was more dressing than salad. Neither of them talked. Fresh roast beast demanded focus, after all.

Their quiet corner of the cafeteria was tucked away under an awkwardly lopsided mural of Monte, the school supposedly grizzly bear mascot. A whole slew of guys from one of the fraternities was hooting and hollering up near the dessert bar, despite one of the cafeteria people scolding them for disturbing everyone else. They were far enough away that the noise was just noise, nothing specific to latch onto.

Leslie shook his head. "Rude."

"Super rude," Ellington agreed as he pulled his dessert to the center of his battered puke green plastic tray. "So, um, English Lit is giving you trouble?"

Leslie blinked at Ellington as if he had no clue what Ellington was talking about. "What? Oh! Oh, yeah. I mean, no, not really, but yes. Sort of? I mean, it's the whole pick a theme thing. We've got four books to choose from and I can't really nail down what theme works best with them or me or both?"

Ellington nodded while licking mashed potatoes off his spoon so that he wouldn't mix gravy with ice cream. "That makes sense. It can be a pain sometimes. Which books do you have?"

Leslie's cheek went flaming red as Ellington licked the back of his spoon.

Ellington stared at him and then did it again.

Leslie went even redder, shifting in his seat like he was having a really hard time sitting still.

"Holy fuck," Ellington breathed.

He leaned forward, cherry pie and melting ice cream forgotten. Leslie went so red that his ears looked like they were coated in scarlet paint. The blush went right down the neck of his seafoam green button-down shirt.

Who wore a shirt like that to the cafeteria? Nobody, that's who. Unless you were on a cheap date, a first date, one where you wanted to impress the guy, but didn't want to look desperate. Ellington made a squeaky duck noise as Leslie groaned.

"You like me!" Ellington hissed at him. "This is a date-date, not a help me pass date! Holy fuck!"

"Of course I like you," Leslie exclaimed just a bit too loud.

They both winced, looking around, but the frat boys were still being obnoxious so no one noticed Leslie or Ellington at all. Leslie leaned forward too, putting his nose just a few inches away from Ellington's. And his lips. His gorgeous, bow-shaped lips that were a bit chapped from being bitten but still perfect in every way.

"Seriously, there you were in shorts for the first time and I thought my heart was going to stop," Leslie admitted like he was ashamed of himself. "You have no idea how good looking you are."

"I'm fat," Ellington complained. "I've got this stupid pudgy belly and my fat thighs and those damned calves are just fat, not shapely. My face is just... round and face-shaped. You're stunning! Oh, my God! Have you looked in a mirror lately? Your abs are like... you could cut steel with those things. And the shoulders, and..."

Ellington spluttered into squeaky duck noises that made a slow grin bloom on Leslie's face. After a moment, Leslie laughed. Totally unfair of him. His laugh was low and deep, the sort of thing that sent a thrill up your spine. Or up Ellington's spine, anyway.

"You like me, too?" Leslie asked, bouncing in his seat like an excited little kid.

"Duh," Ellington said. "God, who wouldn't? Still, date-date?"

"First date?" Leslie said.

He bit his lip, teeth picking at the dry skin in a display of nerves that just about blew Ellington's brain straight out of the top of his skull. Leslie Pherigo, the most gorgeous guy on campus, was outright nervous about talking to Ellington. Because, get this, he thought Ellington was cute.

Holy.

Shit.

"Nope, not first date," Ellington said. He waved a hand when Leslie's glee transformed instantly into dismay. "This is the story we get to tell people when they ask how we got together. Me in my too-early for the weather shorts, you asking for help in a class you didn't need help with. First date should be a real date, not cafeteria food."

Leslie laughed again, slumping back in his chair. "God, you got me going there for a second. Deal. And for the record? I totally could use some help figuring out my theme for the stupid lit class. The teacher is a dragon. She loathed my poetry assignment and kept knocking my grade down every time I revised it. I went from a low A down to a barely passing C by the time I gave up."

"Oh," Ellington said, eyes going narrow. "Her. Right. Well, let's finish up our dessert and head to the library. I know just what you should do to blow her out of the water with your paper. I got your back."

Leslie's smile went two or three notches brighter as he picked up his fork. "Thank you. And if you want to get more in shape, not that I think you need it, I've got your back for that, too."

Ellington's blush flared back to life to match Leslie's fading one. "We'll see. There's time. We can talk about it in a few weeks."

"Weeks," Leslie breathed, stars firmly back in his eyes again. "I love the sound of that. Weeks. You got it!"

They set to eating their dessert, both of them grinning like idiots. Winter might still have a grip on the campus but spring had sure settled into Ellington's heart. Man, what a great ending to the day.

What a great beginning of dandelion season!

AUTHOR'S NOTE: PINK TRUCKS AND BOW TIES

I am not fond of going to bars. I think that shows in this story. They're loud, they're crowded, and you can't hear what anyone is saying. That said, Rahat won't ever be able to claim that xyr trip to the bar was wasted because for once, something lovely came out of it instead of a hangover.

PINK TRUCKS AND BOW TIES

*D*ating sucked. Rahat sighed and stirred xyr drink just a bit too forcefully. The ice crashed against the sides of the glass, not that anyone could hear it. Too much music played far too loudly for xem to make out the ice tinkling. Or xyr date's words for that matter. Wherever xyr date had gotten to.

The bar was dark. Dark and loud and crowded with people more concerned with getting sex than establishing relationships. Rahat's little corner, carefully chosen because xe had a clear view of the front door, the back door, the dance floor and a solid wall against xyr back, felt ridiculously empty.

Perhaps not a surprise given that Ash, xyr blind date of the night, had taken one look at Rahat and put on a plastic smile. Painfully fake, that smile. It didn't reach Ash's pale blue eyes or do more than contort Ash's very pale cheeks.

And that, likely, was what had sent Ash off to hide in a different part of the bar until Rahat gave up and left. As xe was going to do if Ash didn't show up within the next five minutes. Ten at most. Xe truly did believe xe'd been dumped because xe wasn't a thin white young queer with washboard abs and a properly rainbow shirt. Potentially rainbow hair.

No, Rahat was short, stout, dressed in tweed and wearing a very smart red plaid bowtie because bowties would always be more stylish than anything else. And xyr boss smiled when he saw Rahat's bowties. Given that xyr boss was the only thing keeping Rahat in the xyr job at the moment, pleasing xyr boss in any way possible was quite important.

If only Lacey hadn't dumped Rahat when xe came out as nonbinary.

They'd been together for a decade and a half, living quietly complementary lives that lacked everything to do with romance and nothing to do with companionship. Rahat had been quite happy. Not excited, perhaps, but happy. They had their cats, all of which Lacey had taken. Their books, over ninety percent of which Rahat had taken. And between their jobs they'd done well enough to have a very nice apartment with three bedrooms and two parking spots.

All gone because Rahat couldn't stand living in xyr skin any longer, not like that. Not with those clothes and that life and well.

Well.

That was done and over. Rahat was single, probably to stay single for the rest of xyr life and Ash was most definitely not coming back. Fine. At least Rahat could leave the bar before the waitress came around offering Jell-O shots from her mouth for the more adventurous. Xe could do without the teasing that came with xyr spluttering, blushing refusals of such things.

Eleven o'clock and already Rahat was fleeing the dating scene. Xe slipped out of xyr corner, carefully edged through the rising crowds towards the door and did not shout when xe saw Ash animatedly talking with several younger, thinner, whiter queer people by the bar. Yes, with rainbow hair and rainbow shirts and rainbow socks on the one draped over Ash's shoulder. Xe knew it.

Of course, it was raining outside. Rahat glowered at the rain pouring down, resolved to wait in the doorway the five or ten minutes it would take for the wind to switch the rain further to the north. One benefit of living in the Puget Sound: weather always changed rapidly.

"Oh darn, is it raining?"

Rahat turned and started because a very short, very plump woman perhaps Rahat's age was peering over xyr shoulder at the rain. She looked as though she was afraid to even get close to the door. Justified in xyr opinion given that her dressed looked to be made of taffeta. It would spot horribly in rain.

"Wait ten minutes," Rahat said, wincing and then nodding an apology for xyr tone. "It will change soon enough."

"Got dumped?" the woman asked. Her smile was wry but very understanding. "Glad I'm not the only one tonight. What'd you get? 'Don't think we're suited'? Or maybe 'not over my last lover'. That's it."

Rahat grinned despite xyr terrible mood. "Oh no, I got plastic smiles and 'just going to get a drink from the bar'."

"Ugh," the woman groaned with a truly dramatic roll of her eyes. She was quite lovely, if very feminine for a gay bar. "Jeez, have some guts and just say you don't want to try. I hate it when they try that. I've taken to saying, sure, whatever, but if you're not back in five minutes don't bother coming back."

That startled a laugh out of Rahat. "Oh goodness, I believe I will try that next time. A very good suggestion."

"I'm Chandra, by the way," she said with an offer of her plump hand. She had a perfect manicure with lovely white polish topped by little pink hearts.

"Rahat," Rahat replied. "Lesbian?"

"Nah, pan, actually," Chandra said. Her grin was a little stiff. "Pan and aromantic which just makes for lovely discussions with potential partners."

"Huh," Rahat said, actually turning to face Chandra. "I've not met another aromantic before. Nonbinary, bi and aromantic on my part."

"Oh cool!" Chandra said. Her smile became a beaming thing like the sun piercing the clouds on a dreary day. "That's so neat. We should get together sometime and talk."

Rahat was very tempted to say right then but it seemed far too forward. So xe shrugged and licked xyr lips before screwing up xyr courage. "Tomorrow? It is Saturday tomorrow. Or very shortly. I don't think we've reached midnight quite yet."

Chandra laughed. "Tomorrow sounds awesome. How about IHOP? The one on Broadway, down by the AquaSox stadium? Good food, nobody judges and their pancakes are to die for."

"IHOP it is," Rahat replied. "Lunch?"

"Great!" Chandra said. She peeked outside and clapped her hands that the rain had eased off. "I'm going to scoot now, Rahat. I'll see you at noon!"

She pulled her pink jacket, wool by the look of it despite the color, over her dress and dashed out into the drizzle with her hands raised to protect her hair. Rahat stood there for a good five minutes, heart pounding, before xe managed to head out into the night.

A date. Xe had a date with a lovely woman about xyr own age. How in the world had xe accomplished that? Rahat laughed as xe slid into xyr little Hyundai. However, xe had done it, xe fully intended to enjoy the date. It promised to be much better than this blind date had been.

And that was a thing to look forward to rather than to dread.

Chandra checked her lipstick one more time before getting out of her truck. Seriously, there was no reason to be so nervous about this date. Rahat didn't look like the type to get upset about her weight or what she ate or anything. Heck, if anything they'd been quite nice last night.

Of course, last night they might have been drinking and they'd certainly just gotten very rudely dumped so who knew? That might not be who Rahat really was. Which was the reason for an IHOP date. Better to be somewhere very public with nice big open spaces so that no one could catch her.

Catch.

Jeez.

Seriously, she was way too worried about this date. Way too worried. It wouldn't be like Haris. It wouldn't. Haris was an outright jerk and abusive. She'd wanted so much more than Chandra could give and hadn't ever been willing to take no for an answer. Learning experience there. When someone just starting to date you keeps pushing for more and more information out of you, when they won't stop touching even as you try to ease away, don't take that as flattering. It was a warning sign and a very big one.

Rahat hadn't shown a single warning sign. Besides, they were aromantic too. It would be fine.

And if all else failed, IHOP had that special with the cream cheese frosting between the pancakes topped with peaches and whipped cream. Chandra would get a great meal and then run for the high hills.

Worth it right there for those pancakes.

Rahat was already there, no surprise given how long Chandra had dithered over her outfit and then her makeup in the truck. They looked more than a little down when she walked in but perked right back up again when they spotted Chandra by the door. The waitress smiled at her and then grinned when Chandra pointed at Rahat.

"He's been waiting to order until you showed up," the waitress said. "Nice guy."

She bustled off, all teenage energy and whip-thinness, leaving Chandra to make her way over to the booth in the far corner of the restaurant that Rahat had claimed. They really did look decidedly male today. Last night there'd been lipstick and dangly earrings with sparkling stars, plus some very nicely done eyeshadow in golds and browns that had brought the color out in Rahat's eyes.

None of that today, just a shy smile and those big brown eyes staring at Chandra like she was the most beautiful girl Rahat had ever seen. The faint stubble that had marked their chin last night was gone, replaced with a smooth shave that tempted Chandra's fingers towards touching.

"You look good," Chandra said. She waved at Rahat's very nice blue plaid flannel and indigo bowtie. "I love the tie."

And the flannel. Jeez, flannel shirt. A lovely subtle way of signaling that they were queer as a three-dollar bill without being obvious about it. Chandra would love to see what Rahat thought of as formal wear. Tails? Or maybe a very severe evening gown? Who knew? She'd have to find a way to ask later.

"Thank you," Rahat said, tugging the bows a little with such pride that Chandra giggled. "Bowties are always the best sort of ties."

"Totally agreed," Chandra said as she picked up the menu. "They're just flat classy. You didn't have to wait for me to order, you know. I was just dithering over my makeup."

"You look stunning," Rahat said.

They looked like they were going to say more but the waitress came to get their orders. Which turned out to be pretty darn substantial for both Chandra and Rahat. She got one of the combos with the wonderful peach pancakes. Rahat went for the chicken-fried steak breakfast with raspberry compote on their pancakes. Not a bad choice, really, but they came without the cream cheese frosting so nope, not today.

"I tend to go all out girly all the time," Chandra said once they were alone again. And seriously, the restaurant was pretty quiet in their corner, only one really old couple slowly working their way through a seniors' meal together. "My mom was always after me to lose weight, work out, be more 'professional' so now that I'm on my own I dress to suit me. Just not worth it to fuss over whether anyone thinks I'm over the top."

"Absolutely," Rahat said, one hand coming up to their bow tie. They didn't seem aware of the gesture. "My... last girlfriend was always more concerned with what people thought."

"Not serious?" Chandra asked, a little worried she'd be a rebound. Because man, Rahat was so cute. She kind of wanted to go for it even though they'd just met and she was still a bit messed up from Haris. "I mean with her?"

Rahat sighed, staring out the window with an expression was more peeved than heartbroken. "I had thought that Lacey was content with me. We had a very nice apartment together, a comfortable life. We were very good friends. Or I thought we were. She never expressed discontentment at my lack of interest in romantic escapades. But when I came out as nonbinary that was apparently the final straw for her. She insisted on separating. She took the cats. I took the books."

"Not the cats!" Chandra said, clasping her hands to her chest. To her amusement, Rahat's eyes snapped right there. Okay, then, definitely interested in sex at least. And no stupidly complicated dating nonsense to fuss over. "She couldn't take the cats! The beast!"

Rahat laughed, grinning at Chandra. They leaned forward, and it was like the whole room warmed up. Probably just Chandra's cheeks but hey, Rahat was cute. She'd enjoy the attention and see where things went. If it ended up with the two of them in bed together in the very near future that would be terrific.

"I think I got the better half of the deal," Rahat confided. "The cats were lovely, but they fought frequently. Lacey ended up having to give one of them to a friend to stop the battles. Books do not fight."

"Nah, that they don't," Chandra said, leaning on the table too so that their faces were only a few inches apart. "So, what sorts of books you like reading? Fiction? Nonfiction? Bees! Do you like reading about bees?"

Rahat blinked and then grinned at her. "Bees?"

"Bees are important," Chandra said as solemnly as she could.

"And in trouble, I know," Rahat agreed just as solemnly. "I always wished for land to grow an orchard and keep bees though I know nothing about how to do so. Just the thought of it. Plus honey for my tea, you see."

"Oh!" Chandra squealed, clapping her hands.

She launched into her favorite spiel about bees, delighted that Rahat listened with every sign of being fascinated instead of glazing over within minutes. Their food came and they ate, Rahat asking questions about the things she'd said. That turned into her asking about Rahat's hobbies which turned out to be watercolor painting and knitting lace, both of which made Chandra stare at them with utter and complete awe.

"I've never been able to knit," Chandra breathed. The waitress came by with their bill, grinning at the two of them as if they were adorable or something. "Oh wow. You've got to show me sometime. I mean, not how. Something you've made. That's different."

Rahat's cheeks darkened a bit in a blush as they grinned. "I would love to do so. Perhaps, um, another date? I think we should probably go. We've been here more than an hour."

Chandra stared and then looked at her watch. "Whoa. How the heck did that happen? Huh. Well, yeah, another date would be awesome. You want to come to my place for dinner tomorrow? I cook a mean casserole. I was planning on making this chicken, rice and mushroom one my mom used to make. It's super-tasty, no cream of mushroom soup included, too. Real mushrooms and sautéed rice and then it's baked for a good long time until the chicken just falls apart."

"That... sounds delicious," Rahat said with such wide eyes that Chandra started giggling again. "I shall bring a salad and some rolls. I have a recipe for making pretzel rolls that is quite delicious."

"Oh, wonderful!" Chandra said, beaming.

They both contributed a twenty to the bill, covering it and the tip easily. A very hefty tip but Chandra didn't care. The waitress had been very nice, leaving them alone for the most part so that they could talk. Perfect service in her opinion.

Once outside, Chandra took Rahat's hand, giggling at how red they went.

"Gimme your phone so I can put in my number and address, silly," Chandra said.

Rahat blinked and then shook their head before passing it over. Chandra put her info into their contacts, a little embarrassed at being so forward but hey, most of the time she knew whether she could trust someone right off. Even Haris hadn't changed that. She'd known that Haris wasn't trustworthy but she'd gone ahead anyway.

"Um, if dinner goes well?" Chandra said, fidgeting as a

young mom and about six kids rushed into IHOP, the youngest crying about not wanting pancakes. "Maybe... stay the night? I mean, if you're comfortable with that. I think you're super cute and nice and well, we could, you know?"

Rahat blinked and then laughed. "I would be delighted to. I am afraid I am far too used to dating romantic people. To have someone who does not want the romance first is... lovely."

"Seriously," Chandra said. She rolled her eyes over how slow this sort of thing usually went and for no reason at all, really. "Okay, I will see you tomorrow. Six sound good?"

"It sounds perfect to me," Rahat said with the cutest little semiformal bow. "Thank you for having lunch with me."

Chandra giggled, leaning close to press a quick kiss against Rahat's cheek. Thankfully, lunch had wiped out her lipstick because she didn't leave a visible mark. They stood there, hand over their cheek as Chandra scampered away to her truck. Rahat started laughing as she clambered up into the monster-sized thing. Not the first person to react that way and sure not going to be the last because no way was Chandra giving up her big pink truck.

She waved and then drove away, happy, full belly, and already wishing it was dinnertime tomorrow. Man, what a great chance encounter that was. Rahat looked like a super person.

THE SMELL of yeast filled Rahat's little car. It felt so strange to be heading off for dinner with the potential for sex afterwards. Granted, Chandra was lovely and funny and passionate and sweet. But xe had spent so many years learning to fake interest in all the little romantic gestures that to have Chandra cut right past them was quite odd.

A relief, certainly, but still odd. The normal anxiety about how to pretend to enjoy an endless series of dates, the trouble of choosing what sort of flowers or candy or gift to give, that was gone. Rahat felt light, floating without the dragging anchor of all the normal dating conventions.

Free.

That was the word xe was looking for. Xe felt free. After meeting Lacey, they had been friends. Very good friends. They'd more or less accidentally fallen into a relationship, more because people assumed that a woman couldn't simply be friends with a man. Not that Rahat had ever felt particularly masculine but xe'd played the part for years.

It still hurt that Lacey couldn't accept this side of Rahat. Xe had never truly hidden it. Xe'd not said it out loud but xyr love of fine fabrics, 'odd' hobbies like knitting and baking, and pierced ears had apparently not gotten through to Lacey.

How nice not to have to worry about that with Chandra. She'd been so delightful at lunch, chatting and giggling wonderfully. While neither of them could be truly open in such a public place, Chandra had commented that she missed Rahat's makeup of the night before. And that she'd adored xyr earrings.

So, of course, Rahat had put on makeup for dinner tonight and worn another pair of earrings. These had shimmering leaves in gold, silver and bronze suspended from delicate little chains. Xe'd even gone out on a limb and worn a silk shirt in a dusky rose that xe had always thought looked stunning on xyr skin.

Even if Lacey had curled her lip at it and called it 'too gay for words'.

Xe really had to stop thinking about Lacey. It was terribly rude to Chandra who deserved all of xyr attention.

Chandra's house was an actual house set miles outside of Everett. She lived on an actual farm, of all things, with a field that held several cows and a large fenced off garden that lay fallow at this time of year. Rahat stared, slowly driving past the field, and then up to the house where xe started laughing.

Six large beehives stood near the rear fence, quiet at this time of year as the bees hibernated for the winter. Chandra apparently did take her passion for bees quite seriously. Good for her. It was always good to see people living their dreams.

As Rahat got out of his little car, Chandra appeared at the front door, waving wildly.

"Come on in, Rahat!" Chandra said, grinning at xem as xe smiled helplessly at her. "I've gotta pull the casserole. Door's open. Leave your shoes by the door unless they're extra sparkly and pretty. Then bring 'em so I can see 'em!"

She disappeared back inside, leaving Rahat to laugh and shake xyr head. A lovely idea but xe hadn't been brave enough to shop for pumps that would fit xyr feet. So many people would object to that. Makeup, earrings, the occasional flamboyant shirt? That could all be explained as presents for a woman in xyr life. Shoes in xyr size? That was clearly and only for Rahat.

Xe really didn't want to get beaten up, arrested or shot.

The house was a solid little brick building with flowerbeds all around and what looked to be camellia bushes that would give Chandra's bees plenty of pollen. Inside, the house smelled glorious, chicken with the thick scent of rice and mushrooms mixed with a medley of spices that xe didn't dare identify without a taste.

By the door was a bench that Rahat settled on, salad and rolls by xyr side. Xyr shoes came off only to be replaced by a lovely pair of open heel flannel slippers that were quite comfortable. And clearly placed there for Rahat to use because they had a tiny name card on top with xyr name spelled out in Chandra's loopy handwriting.

Rahat followed his nose to the right, finding Chandra in her bright, airy kitchen. The casserole sat on a trivet while Chandra bustled around, gathering glasses and what looked to be homemade lemonade.

"Hey, you found the slippers," Chandra said.

"I did," Rahat said. He gave her a little bow before placing the salad and rolls on the counter. "They are quite comfortable. Thank you."

"Hey, not a problem," Chandra said with a huge grin and a wag of her eyebrows. "I try not to let people's toes get cold. There's so much mud and stuff around this place that keeping shoes by the door is just way easier. Much less cleaning. Your rolls look awesome."

"It is actually a very simple recipe," Rahat said as xe took the lemonade pitcher. "Baking soda and water for the pretzel effect paired with an egg wash for the color and to help the salt stick."

"I gotta get that from you," Chandra said. She waved for xem to bring the lemonade, heading off into a corner of the kitchen that turned out to be a very cozy little dining nook with bench seats upholstered in pink fabric with white hearts. "I don't bake all that much but that sounds really good."

"I am afraid I am a much better baker than cook," Rahat said. "I would hesitate badly before making your casserole. It smells quite wonderful."

They gathered plates, Chandra gladly chattering about what went into it, how it was prepared and several times that her mother had made it. From the sound of those stories, Chandra's mother was not exactly the most supportive person. Actually, she sounded quite terrible.

Pity. Chandra was such a lovely person. Rahat couldn't see why anyone would have a problem with her.

"You're thinking deep thoughts," Chandra commented. She waved her fork at xem, one eyebrow rising.

"I was... thinking that I'd like to scold your mother for her inappropriate behavior actually," Rahat admitted. "Not my place, I know, but she sounds dreadful. I'm sorry that you had to deal with that."

"Man, I'm sorry you had to deal with Lacey," Chandra said while waving away his words. "Seriously, both Mom and Lacey sound horrible. Because they are horrible. And I, for one, am not going to deal with horrible tonight. Because tonight you're here and we have great food and I'm having fun. So the past can just go away."

Rahat stared and then laughed and bowed to her. "I shall endeavor to follow your wishes, then. I hadn't realized I'd said so much about Lacey."

"Mm, not much, really," Chandra said. She smiled wryly. "Just a few 'wow, that sounds like Lacey' comments with terrible things Mom did. Seriously, though, you don't have to avoid talking about her. I mean, she was part of your life. A big part and for a long time. So it's natural you'd talk about her. You don't have to throw away your past with me. I want to know all about you and that includes your life with her. I'm just not the jealous type."

That was a surprise. Every time Rahat had mentioned xyr girlfriends from high school Lacey had been ferociously jealous. She'd rant about them on occasion, ask if Rahat missed them or knew where they had ended up. Xe didn't. Frankly, once the relationships were over, xyr girlfriends had moved on quickly to other lovers and Rahat had never been bothered by it.

They'd both finished their dinners. Rahat was quite full but then Chandra pulled a lovely apple tart from the oven and brandished an ice cream scoop. Of course, all Rahat could do was nod eagerly. Warm apple tart with ice cream? No one in their right mind would say no to that.

"Do you suppose jealousy is part of the romantic mindset?" Rahat asked as xe took the slice of tart and its rapidly melting vanilla ice cream Chandra offered him.

"Seems like it to me," Chandra said very thoughtfully indeed as she rejoined xem at the table. "I mean, every single romantic person I've ever dated has had a thing with jealousy. And the one, two now, aromantic people I've dated have been super chill about it. Like, no jealousy, just honest concern about boundaries and being clear with each other. That's it. So could be. Not like I got a huge sample size though."

Rahat snorted and laughed around his bite of the tart. Which was absolute perfection, warm and sweet apples mingled with a flaky crust, contrasted against the cool ice cream. Truly, if they did begin dating Rahat would have to both practice very strict portion control and get a great deal more exercise.

"This is delicious," Rahat said. "And my sample size is even smaller than yours, I suspect."

"Bought it," Chandra said, pointing her fork at the tart.

She broke into delighted giggles when Rahat made an exaggerated 'oh no!' face at her. The evening progressed much the same, conversation as they did other things. Such as finishing the tart, washing the dishes up, exploring Chandra's lovely little home, and then ending up in bed together where Chandra turned out to be as wonderful of a bed-partner as she was a conversational partner.

Rahat had, logically, brought lube and condoms but Chandra had her own, right there next to the bed. She was delighted to apply the condom herself and very assertive about what she wanted. In fact, she was quite bossy, something that was a joy to Rahat. A woman xe didn't have to do everything for was such a wonderful change.

They collapsed together in the bed, sweaty and, in Chandra's case, giggling. Rahat played with her hair, smiling and happier than xe'd been for a very, very long time. Perhaps ever. Had xe ever had a lover that xe could be completely open with?

Not Lacey. She'd had an image of Rahat in her head and she'd been quite upset when xe didn't match that image. Xyr girlfriends back in high school had been even worse, brief liaisons that were more for public image than for pleasure. So no, xe never had been able to be fully open with anyone xe had ever dated.

"You're tense all of a sudden," Chandra commented. She blew a strand of hair out of her eyes and then frowned at him. "What? I tickle or something?"

Rahat laughed. "Goodness, you're free to try but I am very much not ticklish at all. No, I just realized... I've never been able to be open with any of my lovers before. Not once."

"Okay, that totally sucks." Chandra huffed and sat up, straddling xyr hips with her hands on her hips. It made it very difficult for Rahat to focus, especially with her beautiful breasts right there above xem.

"You're so beautiful," Rahat sighed.

"So are you but no distracting me," Chandra declared. She huffed and bounced a little and then started snickering because Rahat moaned. "Okay, so no me distracting you because this really is important. Paying attention?"

"With all three of the brain cells I have left for verbal communication, yes," Rahat said and then grinned because Chandra snort-laughed, wagging a finger at xem scoldingly.

"Good, use 'em," Chandra said. "Seriously now. I like you. I like you a lot. I'd love to have you move in with me and the two of us spend the rest of our lives together. I mean, I know that's like, you know, super-fast, but you're so much fun to be around and so fashionable and just the nicest person ever. But it's all based on one thing."

Rahat did pay attention, serious attention, because that was not something xe'd expected. Not the 'beautiful' comment nor the rest of it. Xe'd been handsome, dashing, but never beautiful before.

"What is that?" Rahat asked.

"Openness," Chandra explained. She cupped Rahat's cheeks, staring into xyr eyes. "We gotta be open and honest with each other. Not just now but all the time. That's the only way a relationship works. And, I know I mentioned it, but Haris was seriously abusive. Very controlling, the whole roller-coaster of abuse with honeymoon periods leading to escalating tension and violence. I can't go through that again. And the only way to avoid that is to be very, very clear about everything."

Rahat put xyr hands over hers, smiling at her even though xe felt like xyr heart was about to break for her. Another person who needed a very serious scolding. The sheer idea of it, treating Chandra that way.

"I would welcome that," Rahat said, softly, gently, staring into Chandra's eyes. "Truly I would. I have spent too much of my life hiding who and what I am. What you propose sounds like the perfect relationship to me. Though I am not at all sure that I could move in here."

Chandra blinked, snatching her hands away. "What? Why?"

Rahat waved around her lovely bedroom, full of pink and lace and frills. Very full indeed. There were no spaces on the walls left for bookshelves which was a large problem. And her house was so small that xe didn't think xyr books would fit at all.

"My books," Rahat explained and then grinned when

Chandra laughed so hard that she toppled sideways on the bed. "There's not enough room for my books."

She laughed and laughed, cuddling up next to xem and pulling up the covers against the rising chill in the night. Rahat smiled before kissing her forehead. Perhaps xe could give up some of xyr books. A portion of them. Xe didn't need all of them, did xe? But really, xe'd only buy more so it actually was an issue. There needed to be room for growth.

"Not a problem," Chandra finally said. Her grin was a bit hard to see as the evening had progressed to the point that the room was quite dark. Her hug was very, very clear, darkness or not.

"No?" Rahat asked.

"Nope," Chanda said with an exaggeratedly popped 'p'. "This house's got a basement and I've got pretty much nothing down there. Washer, drier, some storage shelves for food, but that's it. Unfinished, too, so you could build it exactly how you want it. Book shelves galore and lots of comfy places to sit if you want."

Rahat sighed, hugging her tightly. "Then perhaps we can discuss my moving in sooner rather than later."

"Cool," Chandra said. She kissed the side of Rahat's neck. "Let's talk about it in the morning. It's late and there's stuff to do tomorrow. I'll do my best not to wake you when I get up to milk the cows."

Milk the cows. Rahat stared into the darkness and then laughed long and hard. Xe found Chandra's face and kissed her hard enough that she moaned into xyr mouth.

"Wake me," Rahat said. "It's been far too long since I had the pleasure of milking cows. My mother would smile to know that I had the possibility of doing it so far from home."

Chandra squeaked and then laughed too. "You got it."

They settled in together, wrapped around each other. How odd, to find a soul that so perfectly matched xyr own after such a crushing date. Rahat sighed as Chandra started snoring quietly against xyr shoulder. Perhaps, when Rahat saw Ash again, if xe did, xe would thank Ash.

After all, Rahat had clearly gotten the better side of that deal.

Xe smiled against Chandra's hair and let the night lull xem to sleep. Tomorrow was another day. A much better day than Rahat had any reason to expect and every reason to look forward to.

AUTHOR'S NOTE: THEOREM OF BRIGHT HALF-LIGHT

This sounds like a SF title. Or maybe an epic fantasy. When I sat down to write this story, I started with that title and my muse veered off at about seventy degrees from anything I expected. Octavia walked on-screen and took over my keyboard in her quest for a cute girlfriend, a fun night, and the best non-alcoholic drink she could possibly get.

THEOREM OF BRIGHT HALF-LIGHT

Octavia raised her chin, pursed her lips and carefully traced her absolute favorite bubblegum pink lipstick exactly around the edges of her lips. It'd taken ages to figure that trick out. Mom made it look effortless, snapping her tube (dark red, matte, worn into an exact match to the shape of Mom's bottom lip) open and dashing it on without even looking in the mirror. Someday Octavia might get to that point but wow, she really wasn't there yet.

Wings with her eyeliner? Now that she had down. Mom always smiled when Octavia put on her wings. She'd look Octavia over, caress a strand of too-thick black hair back into place and then nod.

"You're tall for a girl," Mom always said, "but you really do your wings with such skill, sweetie."

Then she'd nod once more, pick up her purse and spend the entire drive wherever they were going cursing a blue streak at every other driver on the road. For a woman absolutely determined to be classy and stylish at all times, Mom was terrible at controlling her temper once she got behind the wheel. It was sad.

It was always funny to make Mom snarl whenever Octavia said 'Mother, language!' but sad at the same time.

Louisa groaned from the bathroom door as Octavia patted her hair and made sure it was exactly right. "Come on, we're missing the dancing, 'Tavia."

"The party lasts until past three, Louisa," Octavia replied. "Ten seconds to make sure I look good isn't going to hurt anything."

Louisa grunted and looked away. She was still doing the whole grunge thing, dark looks, dark clothes, dark songs unless something anime came on and then she'd squeal and dance like the Louisa who'd been Octavia's friend since kindergarten. Sometimes, not when Louisa was around, Octavia wondered if she'd ever escape her small-town childhood entirely. She'd grown up, moved out of Montana and settled in Seattle.

And yet, Louisa was still her best friend.

The more things changed.

"All right," Octavia said with a nod for her dress, hair and little bag with nothing much more than a little bit of cash, a taser and her emergency tube of lipstick. "I'm ready."

"Finally." Louisa rolled her eyes. "Seriously, all the girls are going to think you're the straight friend, 'Tavia. No one's going to want to flirt with you, much less bang."

"That's because they're going to assume we're dating," Octavia said with a roll of her own eyes. "Come on, everyone thinks we're married."

Which, of course, made Louisa groan loudly. They'd dealt with that for-freaking-ever, as Louisa said. Even back in high school people assumed that they were going to end up together. Silly. Neither of them had any interest in each other, not like that. It'd be like kissing your sister and just ugh. No. Not ever.

Though Louisa did have a point once they left the bathroom. The gay bar was full of women, appropriate for a Ladies' Night, but they were mostly in jeans, flannel shirts and big stompy boots that looked like something a lumberjack would wear. Except far too new for a true lumberjack. Not a scuff to be found on those boots. Made for a really weird look to Octavia's eyes.

Octavia's red and white polka dotted dress with its heart-shaped neckline (all the better to show off the swell of her breasts) stuck out like a sore thumb. No one else had high heels, not that Octavia's kitten heels were that high but hey, she was five ten. Even two-inch heels made her tower over most of the women in the bar.

Which, of course, was the whole point of the dress. Octavia didn't want to be someone's butch lover. She was looking for a butch lover of her own and this seemed like the most direct route to find the girl of her dreams.

Louisa headed straight for the bar, trusting that Octavia would follow along behind her. Which she did, of course, though Octavia's head kept swiveling to look at all the beautiful women as she passed. She beamed at quite a few, got some lovely if puzzled smiles back and then settled at the bar next to Louisa. Who already had a drink with something neon blue mixed with clear liquid that was probably positively volcanically alcoholic.

"What can I get you, sweet cheeks?" the bartender asked, casually shouting over the pounding of the music. She did it with a blatant look down Octavia's dress that was just challenging enough that yep, Louisa was right. She was tagged as the straight friend.

"Your number?" Louisa asked, leaning forward and pushing her breasts together with her arms as she grinned.

The bartender blinked and then laughed. "Nope, sorry, married. How about a drink?"

"Darn it," Octavia replied. "I don't drink alcohol. You have something that looks like a drink but isn't?"

"Coming right up," the bartender replied.

She grinned and winked and whipped up a tall thing with a red layer on the bottom that was just the shade of Octavia's dress. Then the pink of her lips, a creamy white layer and something sparkly gold on top.

"Give that a swirl and tell me what you think," the bartender said.

Octavia did so, stirring it with her straw and then sipping. "Oh. My. God! It's wonderful! So sweet and fruity--I want ten of them!"

She bounced, winked at the bartender when her eyes went straight for Octavia's bust and then looked around for Louisa. Who was over by the dance floor with a similarly grunge girl who was smiling shyly as Louisa shouted pickup lines in her ear.

Oh.

Okay. On her own then. Well, the blatant flirt and bounce thing seemed to work here so off she went to find a nice big butch girl who was looking for a femme to take home with her. It shouldn't be too hard.

Hopefully.

If she had any luck at all, the women in Seattle were better at realizing they were being flirted with than the ones back in Montana. But then when had Octavia had any luck flirting with girls?

ANALISE LEANED against the back wall as Tara and June headed off to see if they could order any wings or sliders or something from the bar. As happy as she was for them, it kind of sucked that they'd hooked up. Okay, not sucked. Tara and June had been head over heels with each other for ages. That they'd finally managed to start properly dating was a good thing. It just left Analise feeling like a third wheel. Fifth wheel?

Whatever. An extra where she wasn't needed. She really didn't know why she'd bothered coming tonight. Sure, Ladies' Night was always nice. No guys hogging the dance floor. Few straights barging in and talking about the queers and how 'interesting' they were.

Just one that Analise could see. Big beautiful girl in a red polka dot dress. She even had some fruity cocktail that she stirred as she smiled at everyone. Pity she was straight. Her hips were gorgeous, wide and round. Big boobs all but spilling out the neckline of her dress. Some sort of multiracial background on her. Olive skin and thick black hair perfectly curled and swirled up into a complicated updo that Analise would love to take down, one pin at a time.

She just about fell through the floor as the woman saw her staring and came right at her.

"Hi!" the woman said in a voice just loud enough to carry over the boom of the music, beaming at Analise.

"Uh, hi?" Analise said. She cleared her throat and projected a bit, deepening her voice so it'd carry better. "Sorry, it's loud. Hi. First time here?"

"At this bar," the woman said. "I'm Octavia. I love your boots. Seriously, they're the first stompy boots that look like they've been worked in instead of polished to death."

Analise blinked, looked down at her worn out, comfy but seriously scuffed steel-toes. Then looked back at Octavia who shrugged, sipped from her drink and then smiled around the straw in ways that made Analise want to seriously ask if she was open to some experimentation. Straight or not, Analise was pretty sure she could rock Octavia's world.

"Work boots," Analise replied with a shrug. "I'm Analise. You can call me that or Ana. I don't care. Here with a friend?"

"Oh sure," Octavia said. She craned her neck and then pointed at a couple of proper goth girls dancing on the floor like they were half a step away from stripping each other's clothes off. "Louisa's over there. She's so good at that. I swear, no one ever takes me seriously when I come to gay bars."

Which. Wait. What?

The question must've shown on Analise's face because Octavia started giggling. She leaned closer, those beautiful breasts almost falling out of her dress. Analise stared for a second and then snapped her eyes right back up to Octavia's face. Rude much? Come on, just because she was a little tipsy was no reason to, you know, perv all over her.

"You're adorable!" Octavia laughed and straightened back up. "So, what do you do? I'm a med tech. It's almost all paperwork. You look like you do real work, though."

"Paperwork is real work," Analise said only to nearly have a heart attack as Octavia caught her hand and ran a thumb over the callouses on her palm. "I mean, not really physical but it's still a good job. Probably easier on your body."

Her cheeks were so hot. So incredibly hot. Octavia didn't seem at all interested in letting go of Analise's hand. That thumb kept on rubbing and it was driving Analise nuts. She knew some straight women liked to play around from time to time, pretend to be bi. Maybe? Or was Octavia bi? That would explain the comment about having been to other bars, right?

Thank goodness, Tara and June showed up right then with a big platter of wings, sliders, chips and dip. Tara stared at Octavia who stiffened and then relaxed when June smiled brightly at her, one hand on Tara's back.

"These are my friends Tara and June," Analise said. "They just got married last month."

Octavia gasped and smiled so brightly that Tara blushed and laughed. "Congratulations! Oh, my goodness, that's awesome. I'm Octavia. I'm trying to flirt with Analise but I don't think she's getting it."

"She wouldn't," June said, the traitor. "She's terrible at picking that sort of thing up."

"Guys," Analise complained, head tipped back and eyes screwed shut against the knowing grins she knew were going to be there. "Come on. Lay off."

"Keep flirting," June said. "She might get it in a month or two. You come here alone?"

That seemed to be all it took for Octavia to make friends because she happily settled in next to Analise, telling Tara and June all about her best friend since kindergarten, Louisa, and her talent for finding girls and getting them in bed with her in a matter of minutes. Which. Analise leaned on their little standing table, munching wings while watching Louisa doing exactly that out on the dance floor. Yeah. She was good. It'd be nice if Analise could flirt half that successfully.

Though Analise still wasn't sure if Octavia was queer or not. Sure, she was smiling and looking Analise, asking all sorts of questions and laughing at whatever stupid things Analise said. She even came back after ordering another of her pink drinks. When she sashayed off to get a third one, Analise leaned closer to Tara.

"Um, is she straight?" Analise asked. "Bi?"

"Dude." Tara stared at Analise like she wanted to smack her through the floor. "She's queerer than a three-dollar bill. And totally into you. I know you're bad at this, but she's just spent nearly an hour showing her tits to you every chance she gets and looking like she wants to haul you into the bathroom for a quick finger bang. Come on!"

"Totally a lipstick lesbian," June agreed. "And totally into you. Don't be an idiot, Ana. Get her number. Ask her out. For real, here. She's dying for it and sending all the signals she can short of hitting you up back the head."

~

Louisa slid up next to Octavia at the bar. Her makeup was all smudged, not that it made much of a difference given how very smoky it was.

"You're looking frustrated," Louisa commented as she waved the bartender down and asked for two beers.

"How do you flirt with a girl?" Octavia whined.

"Honey, just show off those," the bartender, Emily, said. "You'll be fine."

"I've been doing that for an hour now and she still looks at me like she's not sure why I'm here," Octavia almost-wailed. Well, actually wailed but with the music it wasn't wailing. Not really. "Why am I so bad at this?"

Emily blinked, looked over Octavia's shoulder and then snort-laughed. "You've got piss-poor taste in flirting partners, that's your problem, sweet cheeks. Ana's thick as a brick. She once dated a girl for six months and just though they were friends. Came in the day after she got dumped and asked when she'd started dating."

Octavia looked over her shoulder at Analise at the same time as Louisa did. Of course, Analise wasn't looking their way. She was leaning close to talk to her cute little friends Tara and June who really were so sweet and so kind and so clearly amused by Octavia's efforts to flirt with Analise.

"You have such a type, 'Tavia," Louisa groaned. She grabbed her beers while shaking her head. "Here's what you have to do. Go over there. Announce that you're attracted to her and want to Go Out With Her. And make sure you say it's in a very lesbian, very romantic way. Otherwise she'll never get it."

"You're both terrible but I'll do it," Octavia said. She took the lovely Bright Half-Life cocktail Emily offered her and then took a deep breath. "I mean, not even holding her hand and caressing her palm was working. Maybe being all blunt will."

Both Louisa and Emily nodded grimly. Their lips twitched as if they were half a second away from breaking up laughing, which totally ruined the grim expressions. Octavia ignored that and headed back to Analise's side. If the only way she was going to get a lovely butch girl like Analise with her strong hands, steel-toed boots and crew cut was asking Analise out herself, well, so be it.

Octavia headed back to Analise's table with a determined stride. She was almost amused at the way the women in-between got out of her way, some with very wide eyes. The way that Analise snapped up and stared was amusing. Though when Tara shook her head and June gave Octavia a sympathetic look, the amusement went away.

"Uh, should you have so many of those?" Analise asked as she pointed at Octavia's Bright Half-Life. "Cocktails like that usually have a pretty serious kick."

"What?" Octavia's mouth dropped open.

"The drink, it's, you know, probably pretty strong and that's like your fourth one," Analise said. She fidgeted, shuffling her feet and looking so uncomfortable that Octavia started laughing. "What? Your friend is drinking, too. I'd hate to have either of you drive home."

Octavia choked on her laughter and passed the drink to Analise. "Try it. Seriously."

It took three tries before Analise would take it and a very stern look before she'd drink from it. Then her eyebrows went up and her cheeks went as red as Octavia's drink. She passed it to Tara who raised an eyebrow and sipped.

"This is a virgin," Tara said. "Holy shit, I didn't know they made virgin drinks that looked this real. I mean, not here."

"I don't drink alcohol," Octavia said with a little shrug that, thankfully, pulled Analise's eyes right to her breasts. "Emily was nice enough to make it for me after I tried to pick her up and failed."

All three of them stared at Octavia. June started grinning. She offered a fist that Octavia proudly fist-bumped before reclaiming her drink. So. Analise was convinced that Octavia was tipsy. That would explain some of the reluctance. But Tara and June had both made it clear that Analise was bad at flirting. Or realizing she was being flirted with. And Emily had said outright that Analise was clueless about it.

Octavia drew in a breath before reaching out and catching Analise's hand.

"I think you're really attractive," Octavia said. "Very attractive. In a 'I want to date and possibly have sweaty, wonderful sex with that woman' sort of way. And everyone, so far, has said that if I want you, I have to be, um, forthright. So. I want to date you. And have sex with you. Do you, um, want to?"

Her heart just about pounded right out of her chest at saying it that openly. Mom would have cringed and pulled Octavia aside to remind her that proper girls didn't make the first move. Of course, Mother's preferred sort of man was the rich, self-assured type that assumed everyone wanted to date them. All she had to do was be in their presence to get offers. It wasn't that easy when you wanted a lovely butch girl who, if Louisa was right about her 'type', had no clue that anyone wanted them.

"Me?" Analise gasped, staring at Octavia in such shock that, yes, Louisa, Emily, Tara and June were all right. She hadn't realized it. "But, but…"

"Yes, you," Octavia insisted while Tara cracked up, leaning

on June's shoulder as she howled with laughter. "You're wonderful. Just like you are. So date? Yes? No? Maybe?"

Analise stared at Octavia for way too long, her cheeks going redder and redder until she matched Octavia's dress. Finally she ducked her head, smiled shyly and nodded.

"Um, sure," Analise said. "If, you know, you really mean it?"

Octavia squealed and abandoned her drink to fling her arms around Analise, breath catching as Analise caught her and held her easily. Warm and strong and worse at flirting than Octavia was, Analise was perfect.

"I mean it," Octavia declared, giggles welling up as Analise started to beam at her. "We're gonna have so much fun, I swear."

Analise laughed, breathless and shy, but smiling so broadly that Octavia dared to give her a little kiss against the corner of her mouth, leaving a heart-shaped lipstick mark there for everyone to see. Take that Mother, Louisa and everyone else. Octavia had a girlfriend at last.

"Yeah," Analise said, low enough that Octavia felt it more than heard it. Her arms tightened around Octavia just right. "We are."

AUTHOR'S NOTE: THE BILLIONAIRE'S KIDNAPPED BEAUTY

In general, I'm not especially fond of the billionaire romance genre. Real life billionaires are, well, not people I'd ever want to be around, much less romance.

That said, The Billionaire's Kidnapped Beauty was a joy to write. In a collection focused on unconventional romances, Dell and Jyoti were a natural choice. Dell's fierce and tender, running away from a deadly stalker. Jyoti's strong and broken by the losses in her life. Together they created a story that still makes me beam as I read it.

Hope you enjoy the sample!

1. PIKE'S PLACE MARKET

*D*ell hurried through the crowds of Pike's Place Market, sweat dripping down her spine. She'd never been more glad that driving on Pike meant sitting there as hoards of people crossed in front of you, all of them looking at you like you were an idiot. Not that it'd matter for too long. Any second now Radha was going to send his brothers out of his van after Dell and then she'd be screwed.

She had to get out of here. Somehow. While he was trapped in traffic. And too concerned about what people'd think for him to start shouting and brandishing the pistol he'd pointedly shown her when he picked her up for today's 'fun afternoon with my brothers'.

Yeah, right.

Fun.

She'd been blowing him off and letting him down for months but he just wouldn't take a hint. Even Dad having a Very Serious Discussion with him hadn't made Radha leave her alone. No, it'd just made him go all nice and apologetic for a couple of weeks as he sweet-talked Dell's parents into thinking he was clueless and smitten instead of a creep so that when he put her on the spot and asked her out last night, Mom had insisted that Dell go.

He'd waited until they were on the road to toss a ring at her and tell her that they were getting married, right then, that afternoon, because he was sick of waiting for her to make up her mind. Sick of waiting to get to fuck her. So he'd gotten his brothers, the sick little assholes they were, and, slick as all hell, kidnapped her right out of her Mom's arms so that he could force her to get married.

And when she'd said hell no, like any sane woman would, he'd pulled the gun, stared at her and said outright that she'd marry him or he'd blow her brains out and bury her body out in the woods somewhere. His little brother, Derek, had giggled that they already had the grave dug and a real nice front loader to make burying her easy.

Only reason she'd gotten away so far was that she'd flat-out insisted that she needed a bouquet to get married and fresh flowers were the only thing that would do. Not cheap ones, real ones like you got at the Market. Radha had rolled his eyes but he'd driven right down into Pike's Place and then only shouted when Dell dove out of the van and into traffic.

Thank fuck that Saturday afternoons were packed wall to wall on Pike. She might be able to get away, find a phone, get a cop, something.

Dell caught a glimpse of herself in the Beecher's Cheese windows. Her face was way too pale and her hair was a ragged mess flying around her face. She looked terrified. Outright scared out of her mind.

No one around her seemed to notice.

Damn it. No cops in sight. No one that looked even slightly helpful. Just thousands of tourists cramming the streets and hell if there weren't like a quarter of the people around Beecher's as there were everywhere else.

Dell glanced behind and saw Derek heading through the crowd, peering around as if he hadn't spotted her yet.

"Oh shit."

She ran past Beecher's, crossed the street and pushed into the crowd around the French bakery, then past the long, looping line of people waiting for pierogi and then scurried past the people who were ogling the first Starbucks location ever. That put her well out of Derek's sight but she didn't know if Radha had parked. And she'd never see Bam coming. That was his thing, sneaking up on people and slamming their heads into walls.

But if she went past the German Deli then there'd be far fewer people. What she really needed was to get off Pike. Either through the market and down to the waterfront or up east another block into the rest of Seattle proper. If she could do either of those, then she'd be safe. Maybe. At least until Radha found her again.

Dell bit her lip and dodged into the little arcade between the deli and the first Starbucks. Not many people there. Not the best shops, either, soap and knickknacks, but hey, there was a back set of stairs that'd let her get away from Pike Street and she should be able sneak further up until she was well and away.

She was almost to the back exit where the stairs up to the alley waited when she spotted Bam up on top of them. Dell gasped and dove into the soap shop, hurrying towards the back where three really tall, really strong-looking women stood. They all looked away from the massage oil display when she hurried over.

One was Asian, super-elegant and sleek with her hair pulled back and that China Doll makeup that Asian women could do that Dell never, ever could with her dark skin and frizzy hair. Tall, though. Like nearly six foot tall compared to her five three chubbiness. The other one was dark-tanned and stern with rich black hair with the mixed blood wave that made Dell think of the Mediterranean pictures she'd seen. Greece, Rome, that kind of thing. Third woman had bodyguard written all over her and her Black-Latina skin. There was a lump where a shoulder harness had to be hiding which was just what Dell needed right this second.

"Look, I'm really sorry but this guy who's been stalking me kidnapped me and threatened to blow my head off if I don't marry him," Dell babbled to the gorgeous Asian woman. Her suit looked like it was worth more than Dell's entire family's yearly wages put together. "I managed to escape but he's got his little brothers with them and I'm terrified that they're going to catch me."

"Sixteen or so, white as snow and covered with pimples?" the Asian woman asked. The other two flanked Dell, hiding her from the doorway of the soap shop.

"Yes," Dell whispered, throat so tight that the one word came out squeaky. She cringed and hid behind the massage oil display so that Bam couldn't see her when he came in. "Bam. It's Bam. Oh shit."

The Latina bodyguard raised her chin, shifted her stance and put on a glare that could've stripped the bright paint off the walls. Dell didn't quite dare peek but she could just see a reflection of Bam in a glass case full of jewelry a few feet away. He stopped in his tracks, looked around, and then left. Stomping and cursing about uppity bitches who needed a stiff dick.

"He's gone," the Asian woman said. "At least for the moment. My hotel room is just next door. Come back to my room. We'll call the police and get them arrested for this."

Dell stared at her for a stupidly long moment before she managed to stand up. Knees shaking. Hands shaking. Whole body shaking because oh god. Seriously, that was way more than she'd expected when she ran in here.

"I do..." Dell stopped before she could burst into tears. A good hard swallow coupled with digging her blunt nails into her palms kept her from bawling like a baby. "I did intend to get the police. I just couldn't find one before I saw Bam. I mean, yeah, that'd be great but it doesn't need to be your room. Just, you know, an escort to somewhere that I can call for help? They're way bigger than I am and well. White. You know."

All three of the women nodded that they did know. The clerk was watching, listening, but showed no signs of getting involved. He looked like just wanted them to leave more than anything. Dell would've bet her last twenty that he was hung over and miserable.

"I um, yeah," Dell said. "Please. I'm Dell, by the way. I super-appreciate this. You have no idea."

"Jyoti," the Asian woman said. She smiled a little wryly at Dell's surprise. "Third generation. I'm named after my father's adoptive grandmother."

"Oh, okay," Dell said. She gestured at the door. Her hand shook. "Leaving now? Or did you want to buy something?"

"It can wait," Jyoti said. She took Dell's elbow and nodded to her bodyguard to go first. The other woman moved behind them. "Let's go. Laxmi, you're on point. Innes, you have the rear. Don't let anyone get too close."

They went out of the soap shop, up the back stairs and into Post Alley with all the precision and speed of, like, a military unit. Or maybe SWAT. Fast and confident and scary enough that the tourists in Post Alley got right the heck out of their way. A right turn at the top of the stairs, up a quarter block of alley past the little chocolate shop that Dell had yet to be able to afford, then the little kids store with all the cute hats. Laxmi, in the lead, glanced both ways with this super arrogant, super snarly look. Some Danish or Swede or Norse-whatever tourists scattered at the look, hurrying down the steep sidewalk towards the market.

Laxmi nodded once and then Jyoti hauled Dell right out of the alley, up about ten feet and into, holy shit, the Inn at the Market, only one of the most expensive, most exclusive, most impossible dream hotels Seattle had. Dell had never even dared step foot in the atrium, afraid that she couldn't afford to breathe the air.

"Elevator is inside," Jyoti murmured to Dell. "Laxmi, get the concierge to call the police."

"On it," Laxmi said.

Neither of them said a word to Innes who was right behind Jyoti and somehow, Dell had no clue how, guarding Dell's back at the same time. Innes was built kind of like a brick wall, broad and tall and wide, but she wasn't that wide. Just scary like she was.

Inside, the Inn at the Market was classy in ways that Dell had never dreamed of. Soft music, carpet so thick that it felt like walking on air, real oil paintings and Chihuly glass on display where people could touch them. Not that anyone in the Inn looked like they'd touch Chihuly glass. Even the kids look so well-behaved that they'd never scream and run around like little maniacs like Dell used to with her friends.

The concierge was nowhere in sight. Not that Dell was a hundred percent certain exactly what a concierge did or looked like. That was like, maybe, super important butler-person for a hotel? Maybe? Either way, the staff at the desk had that 'I see nothing' expression that Dell knew meant that they not only saw every single detail of her clothes, frizzed-out hair and freaked-out expression but also would be gossiping about it once they were out of sight. Discretely, of course. Because this was a rich person place and you never gossiped in rich people places if you could get in trouble for it.

Elevator went up and up and up until they hit the very top floor. Jyoti kept her grip on Dell's elbow as she propelled Dell out of the elevator and straight towards a door marked not with a number. Oh no, it had a discrete little sign saying 'Beecher's Loft' that made Dell's heart lurch right up to her throat and then straight down to her bladder when Jyoti tapped a key card against the lock and it opened right up.

Innes put her hand on Dell's back, pushing her straight in when Dell's legs locked up at the view.

The incredible, unbelievable, amazing view out over the top of Pike's Place Market to the Olympics off across the Puget Sound. Dell whined. The moment you walked in you were hit by the view. Then by the full kitchen off to the right. There was a table made of red cedar to sit ten people at once time and two big couches covered in leather and oh, holy fuck, a balcony that you could go and stand on while staring down into the street where Radha, Derek and Bam were all still hunting for her.

The penthouse suite.

She'd run up and begged for help from someone who could afford the penthouse suite at the Inn at the Market. Dell couldn't have afforded a closet here. And Jyoti had the penthouse suite to herself. Oh, and her bodyguards. Except maybe not because it looked like the bedroom door was open and there was just one, huge King size bed. So Innes and Laxmi had their own rooms separate from Jyoti and what the hell had Dell done?

"You'll be safe here," Jyoti declared. She strode into the kitchen, pulled open that fridge that was twice the size of the one Mom had at home and offered Dell a bottle of water. "We'll get the police after your... friends. Do you want to call your parents?"

"Um, yes?" Dell said. Her voice went all squeaky. Knees went so wobbly that she wasn't surprised that Innes caught her from behind and push-carried her over to the couch. "Oh, holy shit. Holy shit. Oh my god. She's rich. She's like super rich. I ran up to a super-rich woman and dragged her into Radha's bullshit. Oh fuck. I'm so dead."

Innes snorted as she pushed Dell's head down towards her knees. "Breathe. No one makes Ms. Guldbrandsen do anything she doesn't want to do."

Dell froze. Turned her head under Innes' hand so that she could mouth 'Guld?' Innes grinned for one hot second before going back to the stone-faced stern look. But there was laughter in her eyes and Jyoti was cursing back in the kitchen, apparently on the phone to Laxmi or the cops or something. Dell sighed and just curled up on the couch.

Just for now.

She'd breathe, as ordered, get her nerve back, and then talk to the cops. It'd be fine. Eventually. Once she got over the horror of dragging a super-rich woman she didn't even know into the mess that was her life.

2. ROOM SERVICE

Jyoti cursed under her breath as she waited for Laxmi to pick up. Of all the things to happen on her first vacation since she took over the company. Guldbrandsen Industries wasn't as big or as powerful as some other companies. They made raw materials, plastics of various types, for other businesses rather thing products that consumers would recognize. But her aunt had been badgering her to take a proper vacation for years.

Aunt Hinata would be less than pleased with this entire mess. Not only was Dell poor, she was in danger and likely to bring that danger right to Jyoti's doorstep. Of course, Aunt Hinata found danger the same way most people breathed. She had little solid ground to stand on when it came to safety. Before the last couple of years, it was only her personal assistant, Shelly Sagat, which kept her out of trouble.

Sometimes, even now that Shelly had been fired, Jyoti wondered just how far Shelly had been willing to go for Aunt Hinata. Murder didn't seem unlikely. But she was gone, never to return, so it was irrelevant as Aunt Hinata would say.

She did have a point about Jyoti's tendency to work herself to the point of collapse. The only reason Jyoti had agreed to go on vacation was that she'd literally passed out from exhaustion and a fever she'd ignored for weeks the day before yesterday. The antibiotics were taking care of the fever. Sleep would take care of the exhaustion.

Or it would have before this.

Not that Jyoti would have changed anything from the moment that Dell ran into the Soap Box. Before, perhaps, but not after. Locating a massage oil that didn't have lavender and which didn't have almond oil for her aunt wasn't an easy prospect. Lavender was forbidden because her aunt hated the scent and almond because her aunt was allergic to almonds in all products. No luck yet though some of the merchants in the Market might be able to create one specifically for Jyoti. Tempting thought, that. Aunt Hinata did like things custom-made for her.

None of which had mattered the instant Jyoti had seen Dell's face. The fear had been noted but it was the warm, rich brown of her cheeks, the blush of her lips and the delicate little curls of her hair which spread like a halo about her head that had captivated Jyoti. No doubt, Laxmi was already laughing about how predictable Jyoti was.

Innes, well.

Innes would make her opinion known soon enough.

Jyoti stiffened as Innes strode over, strong, powerful, deadly as anyone in the military or secret service currently. She'd been chosen specifically because she was deadly and because she would not bow to Jyoti's obsessive work tendencies. Between Innes and Laxmi, the amount of overtime Jyoti did had dropped by forty percent in the last month. Not enough for Aunt Hinata but still under sixty-five hours per week. A dramatic improvement.

"She is... having a mild panic attack," Innes murmured into Jyoti's ear. Her fingers squeezed Jyoti's shoulder warningly. "We'll let her rest until the police arrive."

"Do," Jyoti said, flinching a little at the frown wrinkle between Innes' eyes. She didn't know how she could have warned Dell or calmed her down given how little time there'd been but Innes clearly felt Jyoti could have done better. "Hopefully, Laxmi will... Ah! Laxmi, what do you have to report?"

"There's a terrorist threat that's been called in against the Space Needle, Amazon's headquarters and Boing Field," Laxmi said with enough irritation that Jyoti's eyebrows went up. "The concierge promised to keep contacting the police but it may be tomorrow before there are any officers available to assist our guest. Who, by the way, definitely needed our help. I spotted 'Bam' talking to two other men outside the Inn. They clearly are highly dangerous. I suspect that they're white supremists and all three are visibly armed, if one knows what to look for. The oldest of the three looked... hmm. Irate."

"Damn, we need to call her family, get them to safety," Jyoti said to Innes. "See if you can get their number from Dell. I'll arrange to have them transported to safety, put up in a hotel if necessary."

"Yes, ma'am," Innes said.

She marched off, leaving Jyoti to fuss with the water bottle as Laxmi cursed quietly over the phone. Jyoti did her best not to fidget as Innes knelt next to the couch. At least Innes' expression softened as she spoke to Dell. The poor girl certainly didn't need Innes at her fiercest.

"All right, they're moving off," Laxmi said. "I'm following them."

"You're doing no such thing," Jyoti replied, fierce enough to cut through Laxmi's drive to handle everything herself. "I'm going to need you to come back up here so we can save Dell's family. Those idiots will be easy to find. As long as they don't have hostages to hold over Dell's head they're harmless."

"Ah."

That was all Laxmi said but it was enough to make Jyoti grin. Laxmi had always wanted to be more like Innes, a security professional trained to kill, to protect, to investigate, whatever was needed to keep Jyoti safe. What she actually was, was a superlative assistant with the drive to keep Jyoti on track despite Jyoti's too-forceful personality.

"Get up here," Jyoti ordered. "Make sure the concierge has your number and Innes' but get up here."

"Already done on that," Laxmi said. She huffed. "Still rather follow them and get their license plate number."

"Unnecessary right now," Jyoti replied. "Move."

Laxmi hung up, just as Innes nodded and came over with Dell's cell phone in her hand. She was already dialing so Dell must have given her the pass code or opened it for Innes. No sign of Dell, though. Jyoti raised an eyebrow at Innes, holding out her hand for the phone, but Innes shook her head no and kept it.

So. Innes would deal with Dell's family. That meant Dell fell to Jyoti herself.

Not exactly a problem though Jyoti was still too hot from the leftovers of the fever and rather nervous about how well Dell going to handle all of this. The poor, beautiful girl certainly didn't need anyone imposing more restrictions on her.

Innes shoved Jyoti towards the couch. She raised an eyebrow at Jyoti and smirked at the way Jyoti's face went hot.

Damn it. Jyoti hadn't dithered like this since she was a teenager.

Water, a quiet conversation; Jyoti could do that. Even if Dell's lovely face made her brains burn on the bottom from sheer attraction.

"I brought water," Jyoti said, looking over the back of the couch at Dell. Who was curled into a ball on the couch hugging one of the elaborately embroidered and highly expensive throw pillows.

Dell whined and hid her face in the pillow. "I can't afford water."

"...I think it was a dollar a bottle," Jyoti said. She stared at Dell, something like laughter bubbling in her chest.

"You're laughing," Dell huffed as she rolled over on her back to glower up at Jyoti. A moment of glare and then Dell sat bolt upright to grip Jyoti's wrist. "Just how sick are you? What the hell? You're flushed and breathing too hard. What are you even doing out of bed?"

"I have antibiotics," Jyoti protested so automatically that Innes barked a laugh from the very quiet discussion she was having in the kitchen. With Laxmi who'd shown up when? Jyoti hadn't even noticed.

"Sit your ass down, woman," Dell ordered.

She also dragged at Jyoti's wrist, hauling her around the couch and to sit down on it properly, right next to Dell. Her fingers were still locked right on Jyoti's pulse point. The other hand came up to rest, inner wrist first, on Jyoti's forehead. Jyoti groaned.

"Does she have walking pneumonia or what?" Dell asked Innes and Laxmi.

"Really bad inner ear infection that she didn't notice or admit to having for over a month," Laxmi replied. "We knew she was off her game but not that it was that bad. Jyoti's got a history of massive ear infections to the point that she has too much scar tissue to feel when there's an infection. Just feels like pressure."

"I'm deaf in that ear," Jyoti said because Dell's glare was approximately like being flayed alive. "I can't tell by the sound and there truly was no pain. I thought I was just fighting off a cold. I'll be fine. My antibiotics are the most powerful around."

Dell shook her head but she let Jyoti's wrist go. "That's seventeen levels of fucked up, I hope you know."

"No, your 'fiancé' is," Jyoti countered. "I'm prepared to get your parents to a secure hotel to keep them safe from that Radha. Any luck contacting them, Innes?"

"Not yet," Innes said. Her lips were too tight.

"Mom hates answering the phone," Dell said, waving Innes to bring her phone back. "Text works way better. Dad'd answer but he's probably out in the garage working on birdhouses. Makes them and sells them for peanuts at the local Farmer's Market."

Innes and Laxmi both came and waited as Dell texted her mother. Surprisingly given that there'd been no answer at all, her mother replied instantly to Dell's text. Dell was one of those super-texters, thumbs flying as she typed messages out so quickly that it might be a near match to talking to her mother. Her mother must be even faster because after the first text, Dell's phone made a steady stream of tiny bells as Dell's mother texted her.

Jyoti stared. She could type like that but texting that way? Impossible. She'd never managed to figure out the trick of it.

"Okay, Mom's getting Dad and texting my cousins," Dell said, eyes locked on her phone. "My cousins are on the east side of Washington, way out in the boonies. They'll put Mom and Dad up easy. Plus there's a ton of room for their dog to roam safely. Mom says I'm supposed to stay here where its safe until Radha's been caught but man, I don't have to do that. I mean, as long as the cops are on their way?"

Dell looked up at Laxmi who grimaced, then Innes who shook her head no, and finally to Jyoti with a scowl that could have stripped paint. Aunt Hinata would have clapped her hands in delight over it. Jyoti nearly caught Dell's hands to beg her to never, ever stop making faces like that.

So fierce, so beautiful, so everything that Jyoti couldn't resist in a woman.

Jyoti took a breath and then huffed it out again. "There are apparently terrorist threats in against several major landmarks right now. The police are too occupied with that to answer a 'minor' stalking incident. Even one with kidnapping."

"I really hope that fucking idiot gets caught for making fake threats," Dell groaned as she leaped to a conclusion that stunned Jyoti.

"You think...?" Jyoti asked, unable to even complete the sentence.

Dell stared at her. "You don't? Radha was perfectly willing to walk into a courthouse with a gun and force me to sign a marriage license. I mean, he seriously, honestly, for real believed that he could first, get into a courthouse, any courthouse with a gun. And second, he actually, for true, believed that I wouldn't immediately start screaming kidnapping and rape the instant I saw a cop. Come on. Of course he'd be willing to phone in threats like that just do distract the police and keep me from getting help. He's an entitled white-boy asshole who thinks that liking my tits means he deserves to fuck me at will."

Jyoti's mouth dropped open at Dell's rant, part in horror that Radha could be that stupid but mostly in delight at how amazingly beautiful and resilient Dell was. Kidnapped, threatened with rape and death, barely rescued at all and she was already angry instead of terrified. If Jyoti's ear infection wasn't leaving her at half her normal strength, she'd have tried for a kiss.

And probably gotten decked for it, too.

"I'd hope that he isn't quite that reckless but apparently he might be," Jyoti said. "Either way, your family should be safe soon. You're free to stay here for the night. Given my wealth, the police will be here sooner rather than later. If not, we'll call my aunt and she'll enlist the FBI."

"...Your aunt works with the FBI?" Dell asked in a suddenly squeaky voice. Her eyes were like saucers and her cheeks had gone ashy-pale.

"No, she's married to someone who works at the FBI," Jyoti said with a grin. "Uncle Samuel would actually be the appropriate person to call. He's in a supervisory position and deals with situations such as this. The kidnapping, you understand, not the potential terrorist threats. That's his son."

Dell whined and collapsed back onto the couch, the embroidered pillow crammed over her face as she mock-screamed into it. Or maybe not mock given how she curled up into a ball on the couch. Jyoti looked to Innes who smiled ruefully while shaking her head. Laxmi laughed and patted the top of Dell's head.

"You get used to it after a bit," Laxmi said. "Don't stress out, kiddo. Jyoti's just clueless. And stubborn. And relentless. She sees a problem, she's got to fix the problem no matter how sick she is."

"Right," Dell said from under the pillow. She wagged a scolding finger in Jyoti's direction. "You're sick. Go lie down, you. I'm going to just lie here and wait for Mom to call and let me know she and Dad are safe."

"I'm fine," Jyoti tried to say but the pillow shifted enough that she could see Dell's glower. At the same time Innes crossed her arms over her chest and frowned. Laxmi snarled and snapped an imperious finger towards the bedroom. When Jyoti opened her mouth to protest, Dell sat bolt upright and pointed, too.

"Fine!" Jyoti huffed at all three of them. "I'll lie down but you're overreacting. Half an hour, that's it. I'm not lying there awake any longer than that."

Jyoti stomped off to the bedroom, water bottle in hand. Really. She was fine. The antibiotics were taking care of the problem. Sent off to bed for a nap like a toddler, what was the world coming to?

<u>The Billionaire's Kidnapped Beauty</u> is now available at all major retailers in ebook and TPB format.

OTHER BOOKS BY MEYARI MCFARLAND:

Day Hunt on the Final Oblivion
Day of Joy
Immortal Sky

A New Path
Following the Trail
Crafting Home
Finding a Way
Go Between
Like Arrows of Fate

Out of Disaster

The Shores of Twilight Bay

Coming Together
Following the Beacon
The Solace of Her Clan

You can find these and many other books at www.MDR-Publishing.com. We are a small independent publisher focusing on LGBT content. Please sign up for our mailing list to get regular updates on the latest preorders and new releases and a free ebook!

AFTERWORD

The world needs more love. Especially right now with everything that's going on, but always. More love, more lovers, and definitely more unconventional love where the people and their relationships take on forms that differ from what we're all fed by the media.

I've little interest in conventional romances but unconventional love stories are all through my writing. I doubt I'll ever stop writing them, no matter how long I live.

If you want more stories like this, please go sign up for my newsletter on www.MDR-Publishing.com. You'll get updates on whatever I've got coming up, special deals and you can get a free ebook or collection of my short stories. Or you can sign up at my Patreon and get news of any new stuff I publish plus awesome rewards.

Thank you for reading!

Meyari McFarland
    February, 2024
    www.MDR-Publishing.com

AUTHOR BIO

Meyari McFarland has been telling stories since she was a small child. Her stories range from SF and Fantasy adventures to Romances, but they always feature strong characters who do what they think is right no matter what gets in their way.

Her series range from Space Opera Romance in the Drath series, to Epic Fantasy in the Mages of Tindiere world. Other series include Matriarchies of Muirin, the Clockwork Rift Steampunk mysteries, and the Tales of Unification urban fantasy stories, plus many more.

You can find all of her work on MDR Publishing's website.

MORE FROM MEYARI MCFARLAND

Website:
www.MDR-Publishing.com

SOCIAL MEDIA:

Patreon - https://www.patreon.com/meyarimcfarland
Mastodon – https://wandering.shop/@MeyariMcFarland
Pillowfort - https://www.pillowfort.social/Meyari
Facebook - https://www.facebook.com/meyari.mcfarland.5
Pinterest - https://www.pinterest.com/meyarim/

IF YOU ENJOYED THIS STORY, **please leave a comment on your favorite site. Also, please sign up for the newsletter so that you can hear about the latest preorders and new releases.**

www.ingramcontent.com/pod-product-compliance
Lightning Source LLC
LaVergne TN
LVHW041641060526
838200LV00040B/1664